Poe's Women

C. F. Dorn

POE'S WOMEN
by C. F. Dorn

Copyright © 2019

Published by Echo Arcade

Printed in the United States of America

ISBN: 978-0-578-57115-7 (paperback)

*The boundaries which divide Life from Death
are at best shadowy and vague. Who shall say
where the one ends, and where the other begins?*

—Edgar Allan Poe

The number of our doubles is infinite in time and space.

—Louis-Auguste Blanqui

FOREWORD

FONDLY CALLED "THE SPRING GARDEN HOUSE" the residence at what is today 532 North 7th Street and Spring Garden in Philadelphia once housed the family of Edgar Allan Poe, "America's Shakespeare."

Sometime early in 1843, Poe, his aunt Maria Clemm and her daughter, Edgar's 'child bride,' moved into this brick, three-story structure which was easily twice the size of any home the trio ever lived in, a relatively new dwelling built only the year before.

Poe moved here into a quiet Quaker neighborhood because it was not only more of a country-like setting for his wife's fragile health, but the city had become increasingly violent. He was always protective of 'Sissy,' even moreso now since she had become ill.

By the time Virginia, Maria and Edgar—and the family cat, a tortoise-shell tabby named Catarina—came to Spring Garden, Virginia was clearly in a mode of partial invalidism, more or less typical of consumptives during this time, a disease that would claim her life five years later, at the age of 24. The idea of return, either in essence, or in one's earthly image, occurs continually in the fiction and poetry of Edgar Allan Poe.

The early drafts of "The Raven"—the poem that would create for him international fame—were first penned in the small study on the second floor of the Spring Garden House. It was here that Poe still pursued the establishment of a literary journal, *The Stylus* and by May of 1843, his backers had withdrawn from their contract. It was for him then, and would remain until his death, "the one great purpose of my literary life."

Even though Poe's Philadelphia was a burgeoning commercial center, its inhabitants shared beliefs commensurate with the 1840's. The world was still a mystical place. Secret societies, necromancy, the black arts, brotherhoods devoted to the occult, all flourished. The countryside had greater curative powers than hospitals or physicians. Windows were closed to night spirits. During a period that preceded the age of electricity, there were hundreds of thousands of stars visible to the naked eye each night ready to confirm the reality of a heaven above, a true firmament. Night birds carried messages.

It has been suggested that Poe, during his final days, was considering a return to Philadelphia. The house still stands. It is a national historic site, staffed by the National Park Service.

In this narrative, two original manuscripts of Edgar Allan Poe, hitherto unknown, are presented here for the first time.

—The Editors

THE FIRST DISCOVERY

*A*fter all the excitement that night, I quickly fell to sleep into a
kind of stupor and only came around hours later when I heard
a commotion in the other room.

*It was Reynold, opening up the place. He had arrived for his shift.
The light was just coming in the windows and it was early, even for him.*

*"Dorn?" he said standing outside the reading room in his Mummer's
costume, with those exaggerated neon-colored feathers in his headband,
still in make-up, he must have come directly from the station where he
was working with his division, putting the final touches on the routines
for the upcoming yearly parade.*

"I think you should see this," he said. "Come around to the back".

*By the time I straightened up the sofa, folded and stored away
the blanket, and joined him at the rear of the house, he had already
changed into his government uniform, the olive-green pants and jacket
of the National Park Service.*

The body lay in a heap on the wooden storm cellar door.

*It was that of a young female. She wore a tight-bodiced chemise with
puffed sleeves. A woolen shawl lay in a pile. Her hair was dull blond, fine
as it was profuse, tied in a bun with a blue ribbon.*

*Reynold stood over the body. "I was afraid it would come to something
like this."*

A thin necklace of red, like a ruby choker, ran under her chin. Reynold squatted down to examine it without touching the corpse. The head itself was askew, oddly twisted. Reynold removed something that had been tucked in her waist scarf, which matched the material of the ribbon in her hair. He carefully unfolded it, and scrawled in crude pencil was the following:

> A bright loss, more or less,
> But consider this,
> With Pride there is such pain,
> Eternal pain & anguish,
> More with less, & always this—
> Love, will any love remain?

He took the note. "This should interest the authorities."

"Shouldn't you tell him first?" I asked.

"Him?"

"Yes, you know, Poe. Shouldn't you be telling Poe," I heard my voice rise.

"He already knows." Reynold looked up at me, and for a moment appeared to study me somehow, as if something was not understood.

As much as I wanted an explanation then and there, I knew the house would soon be overrun with police.

I returned to the reading room to get my backpack and the few necessities it contained, so I would not be there when they arrived, and no one would know I spent the night. I wanted to give my farewell to Reynold, but when I came around to the side of the house, expecting to find him still with the body, he was not there. And the corpse, the beautiful young woman who lay crumpled on the slanting storm cellar doors only moments before, was gone.

ONE MONTH BEFORE

Before I met her, and she tricked me into thinking we were in love, before I knew how close she was to Reynold, and Reynold to Poe himself, and how the two of them worked together to help Poe in his quest, before I slipped out of my body like a suit of clothes, or saw the murdered girls, one by one, I could have avoided it all. There was a moment I had the chance—the only chance—to walk away from it. How often do we suspect, if ever so slightly, and if only for a moment, that our senses are telling us to turn away from something and we pursue it anyway? If the senses were there, they were not strong; if they were insisting I act differently, I wasn't listening—or couldn't.

It was the last day of the conference and the afternoon sessions were dragging on interminably. After I found myself nodding off, more than once I got up, walked around, then slipped away to the coffee shop in the hotel lobby.

When my name was called, I stepped forward to claim one of the two cups on the counter; chose one randomly, then just as I saw it belonged to someone else, a voice off to the side said, "I'll take that—unless your name's Alana." She seemed amused, and when she noticed I was holding a leather briefcase, she assumed I was attending her literature conference.

"No, sorry," I said. "I'm with the National Holographic Studies Association—the other side of the building."

Her eyebrows went up. "And you're in what again?" she asked.

"Experimental imaging," I said.

It was her last day as well, and as it turned out, we were both escaping the very last sessions which usually feature the worst speakers, and the entire conference had become what conferences usually become when they go on for days, oppressive.

We were both scheduled to fly out the next day. While Alana visited the city often—one of her relatives lived there—and knew the historic sites and landmarks, it was my first trip to Philadelphia.

She said she would be willing to show me around—she actually said she could be "talked into it," but only when we had more time. That meant she expected I would be back, when I had no intention of ever returning. It wasn't that I didn't care for the place, I'm just not one for tourist attractions, and I'm behind in my political history, something I've neglected over the years. My enthusiasms, and all my energies seem to have gone into my interests which are all connected with the unrelenting demands of my work.

She held up a canvas bag, the kind one finds in grocery stores that specialize in health foods, to avoid use of paper and plastic.

"Look, I have to drop these off to a friend. It won't take long. Want to come along?" She opened the bag to show me.

It was the end of November, and it was getting on toward the end of a winter's day. The sky was gray, and in two hours it would be dark. "I really don't think we have much time," I said.

"C'mon then, we'd better hurry," and took my hand, leading me out the door. Before she visited her friend, she wanted to drop by a tavern on Chestnut street, a brisk walk, a few blocks from the hotel.

"Guess why I wanted to come here?" she said, removing her coat and giving it a shake soon as we came through the door. "Because we are in the heart of the publishing district. Just down the street there—" she pointed in the direction of the Delaware river—"was the *Lady's Dollar Newspaper* and *Godey's Lady's Book*," then turned on her heel, "and that way, on the next block, was *Graham's Magazine*, where Poe worked."

Alana was an 'Americanist' and taught in a small college in the Midwest. As she went on, animated with her subject, I couldn't help noticing her eyes; they were pale gray, the palest gray I'd ever seen. She stopped only when the waiter arrived.

"This is Marcel," she said. "He's from Belgium, isn't that right, Marcel?"

"Exactly," he tapped his pencil on his order pad once, then looked about as if impatient.

"What would you like this afternoon?"

When Alana asked for a recommendation, he became more agreeable. "Well, of course, always the Orval," explaining it was among the oldest of Belgian brews, and added with some pride, "I grew up on it."

Alana looked at me. "Two then?" But I didn't feel it was necessary to respond at that point. I felt the order, like Alana herself, was out of my hands.

"Marcel and I know each other," she offered. "We were lovers—once," and looked up coyly.

He became impatient again. "Will there be anything else, then? No? If not, excuse me. I must see to my other guests."

Soon as he left, Alana continued, "During the early 1840s, Poe was in this area almost every day. He could have been in this very building, stood on its floors, lingered in its rooms, long before it became 'Eulogy,'" she said of the tavern's contemporary name, "after it was a home to other businesses; an accounting firm, a bookstore owned by a publisher, even a jewelry shop." She seemed mildly pleased with herself, smiled, rested her elbow on the table, her chin in her palm, almost as if posing as a child might pose, a girl, as if she—or I—might find that attractive somehow.

Marcel brought the heavy glass schooners, and we were not halfway through, when Alana reached across the table. "There's someone I want you to meet," she said.

"You mean someone like Marcel? Another lover?"

"No," she laughed, "not another lover. He's much too old. He's a dear friend. You'll like him, besides, I have to drop these off," she held up the bag of books again. "He's been waiting for them.

We were on our way to the Independence Information Center to meet Reynold, who worked as a temp whenever one of the regular employees was ill. He had another job, a full-time one, which allowed him to occasionally fill in for other government workers.

There were snow flurries blowing around in the air, and I noticed immediately the temperature had taken a steep drop. After walking more than a half mile, we were glad to be in a heated building.

Reynold was seated at a long counter, bent over some papers. The place was nearly empty. There were a few employees wandering about, but the tourists were gone.

When he saw Alana approaching, he removed his glasses—he had them attached to one of those beaded chains—and put his arms out. They both embraced over the counter between them. They chatted a bit. She whispered something in his ear, then introduced me. He was pleased he said, of course, to meet someone in a field he found "fascinating," and "admirable" with all its "great technological advances," at the same time, he was gathering up the reading materials at his station. He apologized. It was almost closing time.

"I thought I would take Dorn,"—she used my last name for some reason, dropping the first and middle names, something for which I was grateful—"over to the Spring Garden house, since he's here anyway," Alana said, tilting her head a little as if to say, "What about it, Reynold?"

"It's much too late," he said, checking his watch. "By the time you arrive, they will have closed." He pulled a metal cord with a key ring from a round leather holder attached to his belt, twisted out a key, and pressed it in her hand. "Here, this should help. But I warn you, you go at your own risk. Hurry now, the storm is coming on."

Alana protested, "No. I can't take—"

He interrupted her, "I have a duplicate—"

"But I may get you into trouble." I took this as a reference to entering a government building after hours; what amounted to an unauthorized access to a national historic site.

"Nonsense," Reynold replied. He offered to call a taxi, in fact he insisted on it, even as we rushed out of the center, down the concourse to the street.

Alana knew the way. We could walk it easily. She was confident. It was just over a mile but we had not reached the end of the block, we had not turned north on 5th which she knew was the most direct route to the historical site, when I realized it had become dark while we were inside speaking with Reynold, and the streets were now empty.

For a moment—and it was only a moment—I was entirely alone, the only occupant in a void, abandoned there by forces I did not understand, or could I control.

The news of the anticipated storm kept would-be travelers indoors. The snow was falling freely now, heavily enough to obscure our vision. I could barely see the distant traffic lights.

We had not reached Arch Street, when some temporary road construction caused us to detour from the original route. From then on, it was a series of miscalculations. Alana knew a short cut, and we went down several side streets, all the time, the wind picking up and the snow, approaching blizzard-like conditions.

My sense of apprehension began to grow when we walked through what seemed to be a warehouse district. It was here Alana finally admitted we had strayed from our course, that she no longer knew where we were, or a route of return. We were walking quickly now; I could feel the sharp air, like a clot, at the base of my throat every time I breathed. How could we have gone so far out of our way? We passed rusted iron doors, buildings with broken windows, and the sense of absence—I saw no one—not a soul, and at times had to look around to make sure Alana was actually there. She was bundled in her dark coat, her head bowed, silently shuffling along through the ankle-deep snow. She could have been a form out of my own imagination at that point, which only added to my sense of absence now greater than that of people or things—it was complete, a total desolation, beyond anything I could ever describe.

My extremities—fingers and toes—had gone from a tingling sensation to numbness, to not experiencing any sensation at all. There was an increasing concern that, alone as I was, or felt I was, at any moment some menacing thing could appear from those narrow alleys that separated those 19th century buildings. I assumed the warehouses were abandoned, but nothing that large is left alone for very long, and the feeling—it was very clear—that someone was lurking about was always with me, even after we passed through that blighted area.

When we finally arrived at a corner, with drifts about the street sign, I strained to make out the lettering. Everything was screened out in white. We tried to locate traffic lights—these had served as dim markers before—but saw none. We had either wandered so far we had come to the edge of a rural area, at an intersection of a country road, or the snow had enveloped the signals, or what was most likely the case; there had been a power outage.

Lost to any sense of direction, we continued on for some time, knowing movement was our only hope, and to stop—for anything—would only prolong our situation, or make it irretrievably worse. As we moved along this way, locking hands, thinking we were going forward somehow to some recognizable destination, we saw in the far distance two yellow lights, and above them, a revolving beacon. I ran ahead, and when I saw it was a snow plow, waved my arms, and tried to shout, but the air, heavy with moisture, and the silence snowfall brings, absorbed all sound instantly.

In my enthusiasm to get out onto the road, I tumbled over a bank of snow, and as I did, the lights slowly turned, then swung out of view.

I lay there stunned for some time, thinking we had missed any opportunity we may have had to find our way back. It was a relief, somehow; the cold, now strangely more of a comfort than the hostile thing it had been, and just as the stillness was gathering around me, I heard Alana say, "Look, it's coming around again." The big machine was behind us now, its curved blade turning over the thick white layers and rolling them off to one side, the eyes of its headlights beaming ever closer.

We worked our way to the edge of the street, and stood in a knee-high drift, waving to the steel beast as it approached. It was white itself, and Alana remarked that the vehicle resembled "an oblong box." She seemed amused by her observation.

The driver did not see us until the blade was with a few yards of us, and he pulled the vehicle to a halt, sprung the cab door and beckoned us over. We climbed up into the truck, out of the blizzard, and sat on the stiff, cracked vinyl bench seat.

He wanted to know where we were going, and when we told him, he shook his head, "You're miles away. There's no way of getting you back that I know of. Not tonight," and offered to take us along—he was finishing his shift soon—and would try to get us back as close to the hotel as possible. With that, we huddled together, while the truck crept along one street after another, finally working its way toward Front Street which was cleared, and down to Dock Street, right around the corner from the hotel.

The lobby was filled with hotel guests. When the power went out, so did the elevator, and after the electricity returned, the elevator was still locked. The hotel management set out complimentary wine stations for its patrons, some of whom either had difficulty getting up to their rooms and were waiting for the elevator to begin operating again, or had been out earlier, and were now swapping storm stories.

We stopped by one of the wine tables for some of the house's hefty Merlot, and with our glasses in hand, went outside to take the emergency staircase up to the fourth floor, where Alana was staying.

I thought I should see her to her room, although when she assured me it was not necessary, she was a bit coy, almost inviting. Alana slid her pass card into the door and said, "Come in. I'll show you what you missed."

She opened her laptop and with a few key strokes brought up images of the poet's house. It was a little tour; she took me from this room to that, explaining everything, as if all of the information was important somehow, and I had the feeling, she expected me to think it was important as well.

Image after image passed by, attended by her detailed descriptions, and I was simply taking them in with as much interest as I could manage, when I asked her to stop.

"Could you scroll back?" I asked. As she did, I said, "There. What's that?" I was looking at a dark object, very large, like a public sculpture one finds so often in older cities.

"It's a statue of Poe's raven. Big, isn't it? I think it's bronze, but the weather hasn't treated it kindly," she said referring to the darkening patina of the metal. With its great beak open, and its wings outstretched, it looked ominous to me, like a predator. It stood outside Poe's house as if protecting it.

I went down to the lobby for refills, and when I returned, we sat on the edge of the bed, Alana going on about the residence. Eventually, with the vital facts exhausted, we laid back, staring at the ceiling, our feet dangling over the edge, recounting the events of the day, sometimes with humor, glad to be safe once again, out of wind and snow, and slowly, we began to drift off.

I knew I should be leaving, but couldn't bring myself to say so, thinking all the time it was the extreme tiredness that was preventing me, and I began to dream, or thought I was dreaming. Alana's face appeared above me, much as it had in the tavern, and her eyes, their pale grayness, seemed at times, to flash quickly as if silver, then disappear. I woke once or twice, or thought I did, then fell back to sleep just as quickly.

The next thing I knew Alana was coming out of the bathroom, wrapped in Terrycloth, vigorously drying her hair. It wasn't yet dawn, and the day would soon open with an overcast, gloomy sky.

She had to leave, she explained, "Early flight," and came over to the edge of the bed. "Would you see that Reynold gets this?" she asked, taking my hand and placing the key there, then kissed me on the forehead.

I was not scheduled to fly out until later in the day, and assuming the streets had been cleared, I had time to take a taxi to the information center.

"No, not there," she said. "Reynold should be at the Poe house. It will give you a chance to see it," she smiled. "He works there as one of the park service's curators. He's been there a long time," she added.

*   *   *

I stood across the street in the cold, looking at that ominous great metal bird that stood like a protector of that house and all that was in it, the raven I had seen on Alana's computer screen the night before. This was the moment when I could have turned back, as if half of me wanted to leave, while the other half wanted to walk across that street, and in another moment it seemed it had already crossed, and stood near that statue, waiting for me to join it.

Often I've read about the impression of place, the profound affect physical locations have on people, but I never experienced anything like it, not until now, standing motionless across the street from the doorway of a building I knew I would enter when everything seemed to tell me otherwise. I watched myself, a complete figure in my own coat, staring back at me, as if I were being summoned, but it was more than that, I was compelled, drawn to that house beyond any ability to resist my other will, the will that told me simply to leave. The next thing I knew, I had joined myself, and became the shape that was waiting for me.

In another moment I was walking up those few steps to the entrance, twisted the brass knob as if I could open the door. Every visitor finds it locked. The attendants keep it that way so the caller must use the heavy door knocker, even then no one answers imme-diately, and the guest must wait. This builds suspense; adds to the gothic drama of the place, intentionally staged by the keepers for the benefit of the patrons, but it had no effect on me. I was not amused, or made wary by this theatrical ploy. My concern went deeper. I was being led against my will to enter a place where I knew, once I stepped across its threshold, everything would be changed, and changed irrevocably.

The attendant was pleasant enough, and soon as he let me in, returned to his station behind a desk in a reception area featuring broadsides, replicas of Poe's poems on imitation parchment with his reproduced autograph, pamphlets, postcards, posters, Poe T-shirts, and other memorabilia tourists could purchase.

When I asked to speak with Reynold I was told he was upstairs with a tour group, and when he was done, he had an errand, but if I was patient I could see him eventually. I was shown to a view-ing room to see a little documentary film on the life of the author, a complimentary gesture for visitors. Left alone, I was becoming increasingly agitated, as if I was supposed to do something, perhaps a task of some sort, but knew not what. There I sat, waiting for Reynold, enduring several showings of the short film. Once I heard voices in the hall, and as I opened the door to see if Reynold had returned, saw no one. The voices seemed to be carried off—down the hall, up the staircase.

I wandered around a bit, peeked downstairs into the cellar, looked into the parlor, and all the time heard the voices going on upstairs. When the group was guided back to the reception area, it was not Reynold who led them, but rather another park service guide.

It was becoming dark again. I went to the reception desk to ask about Reynold once more, but it was unattended. After a few minutes, I used the 'phone on the desk to call for a taxi.

My flight had left hours ago, and I did not think, not once, to reschedule. Instead I took dinner at Eulogy tavern, and afterward, wandered back to my room.

The next day I visited the house again. There was a different attendant who said Reynold was sorry he had missed me, but had left something, and from under the desk pulled up the bag of books Alana had given him. "He said you should read these. They must have met with his approval," he smiled. "Reynold said you would have time." Again, I was informed the subject of my search was absent, and if I kept returning, would eventually meet up with him.

I thought I might leave the key and be done with it. Something prevented me, something more than leaving a valuable object in the hands of a stranger, or possibly risking Reynold's position.

Over the next few days I remained in my room reading the contents of that bag: several biographies of Poe, a book of timelines—his comings and goings—his publishing transactions, a dictionary of associates who were important to him personally and professionally, a complete collection of his works—critical reviews, a novel, stories, poems—and a long treatise on the universe he had written after the death of his wife which I reread several times during the course of the week, all the while wondering why Alana hadn't given them to me herself. Apparently she had to pass them by Reynold for his review; that they would be sufficient to give me what I needed to know about Poe.

Meals were taken infrequently, with an occasional walk down to Chestnut Street to that Belgian beer tavern, then sitting there for hours. If I was lucky, I could get the little table by the window, and when I wasn't reading, stared out at the street and the people who came by, all the time wondering why I was still here, still in Philadelphia.

My employer contacted the hotel for several days and left messages. These went ignored. The company—Global Spectrum Enterprises—had called so often asking about my whereabouts that I finally informed the desk to tell them I'd checked out, that I was no longer available, anything to discourage them. They had made a sizeable investment, not only in me, but in future projects in which I had a role.

I was so taken with a sense of obligation to my new business, which I did not yet fully understand, that I neglected myself. My clothing went unchanged, and when I looked in the mirror, I realized a growth of beard was coming in, although I never went without shaving, never a day, not one since I first began the daily routine.

Despite my emails and texts, I heard nothing from Alana and began to think she had forgotten me. Had I returned to that little Belgian bar because she was missed? In her absence, had I grown fond of her, or more than fond? Maybe in a fantasy I imagined, I would stumble into her, that she might be there waiting for me as if she had never gone.

One afternoon Marcel came around as I was finishing lunch. "Did your friend show you the city?" he asked.

"You mean Alana? No. We were prevented by the storm."

"Ah, yes. The storm," he smiled. "Can I get you anything else?"

I wanted to ask him more about Alana. When this thought occurred to me it was followed by an uncomfortable feeling. If I asked, maybe I would hear more than I really wanted to know. "Actually," I admitted, "I've been trying to get in touch with her, but haven't been able to."

"She's like that," he said. "Sometimes she will be very responsive, then you won't hear from her for awhile. But some people are like that. Don't you find that is true?" he said, clicking his pen.

"Yes, I suppose."

"They give you some attention, then go off by themselves and do whatever they want to do. Does it trouble you?" he smiled again.

"No, not at all," and at that point he reached over and cleaned up the table. It offered a convenient point for me to end the conversation and leave the tavern.

On returning to the hotel I stopped at the registration desk to renew my room only to learn my credit card was no longer valid; my account depleted. I hadn't returned Reynold's curator's key although I had often stood across from that historic house, staring at the old brick building and the giant metal raven; reluctant to cross the street and enter the place again.

I was doing just that one afternoon, and not having the fare for a taxi back to a hotel whose management was not agreeable—even after some pleading on my part—to extend my stay for an extra night until I could settle my credit card situation, when, walking away from the site, I stopped at a crosswalk and there next to me, waiting for the light to change, was a vagrant.

"You look the poorer for it," he said.

I had no intention of engaging him, but he kept staring. Finally I asked, "What? The poorer for *what?*"

"For whatever ails you," and held out a soiled hand which I ignored. "Skrimp," he said, "that's me all right all right." He looked me over again. "You need a place to stay do you?"

I admitted I was falling behind a bit with my financial obligations at the hotel, but still felt it necessary to remain in the city. It would only be a matter of time until the misunderstanding about my account would be straightened out.

"Get your things and meet me back here. I can do a favor for a stranger. Skrimp can."

My business, whatever it would be, was not finished, and until I learned of my purpose, I could not leave. Along with my luggage which I no longer needed, I had brought a back pack with conference items which I discarded, and filling it with my things, I returned to the spot where I had met Skrimp. Eventually he showed up. It was dark, and I could barely recognize him. We walked together for some distance, then turned down a street almost randomly, and I realized I was again in the district of abandoned warehouses.

We went between two buildings, down a flight of broken concrete steps, and Skrimp pushed aside a large piece of plywood that had been guarding an entrance way.

"Here we are we are," he said with pride pointing out an area that could have been an abandoned cellar storage room once used for cleaning supplies.

"You'll be warm here," he said. "Out of the wind all right."

It was obvious the place had former tenants. The telltale signs were everywhere: empty bottles and other litter of former inhabitants were scattered about the centerpiece, a stained mattress set on flattened-out cardboard boxes.

Skrimp did not return for several days. He did show up the morning after the disturbance, a fitful night in which I found no sleep at all.

It was very late, and as I began to doze off, I heard a commotion taking place somewhere in the building: distant voices—proclamations of some kind were being made. These were forceful, direct, as if from a creed, followed by chanting, and then sounds of agony. The cries followed a slapping sound as if something was striking human flesh. This continued for some time then eventually died out, and the place was silent once again.

When Skrimp came around early the next day, I asked him about the goings on.

"Gangs," he said. "That's all. Keep yourself out of it. Block your door. There's lumber around here. Use it. You'll be all right all right."

But that wasn't true. A few days later, the same sequence of events occurred again. This time, Skrimp was no where to be found, and when I left my building to step out into a dull morning, one without movement, overcast, facing me were two boys in their late 'teens was my guess, maybe as old as twenty, staring intently at me soon as I came up the stairwell. They wore caps and suspenders.

"What do have down there?" one asked.

Before I could answer, he brushed aside me and went to inspect the storage area where I'd been staying, while the other remained to obstruct my going. He carried with him a lengthy white shaft, perhaps bone, the kind used for canes, shiny as if it had been polished by use and age, embellished with some carved designs I could not decipher.

When his companion returned agitated—he could find nothing of value—I was thrust up against the building, my back pressed flat along the brick surface and that white rod across my throat.

"You're *not wanted* here. This is no place for you. Understand?'

Unable to speak, I nodded to agree.

He pressed tighter and it occurred to me that I might pass out, that with a bit more pressure the trachea would be crushed and I would be left for dead.

One looked at the other as if they shared the same intent, as if they were giving each other permission to execute me on the spot.

At that moment, when I knew my demise was certain, and I had shut my eyes as if to close out the inevitable, there was a shout from down the alleyway. They both turned, and seeing what demanded their attention, immediately fled.

It was Reynold, accompanied by two other men. As he hurried toward me, his companions ran on ahead, pursuing my assailants.

"We've been searching for you for days," he said, and looked disgusted as he scanned the derelict building, the gang graffiti that covered the wall inside the stairwell, and finally at me, at what I had become.

"I believe those young men," I said, "were trying to kill me."

"Young men?" he repeated. "They're thugs. Felons."

"Will they be caught?"

"Possibly. But my guess is they know this area better than just about anyone, and can slip around these abandoned places well enough to dodge any possible captors, including my colleagues."

"Why me? I have nothing of value."

Reynold shrugged. He picked up the key lying on he ground. It must have fallen out of my pocket during the scuffle. "Maybe they were after this," he said. "Or maybe they just wanted you out of the way. You may be more valuable than you know. Whatever they have in mind, you obviously were not meant to be included." With this, he brushed back the side of my jacket and dropped his curator's key into my shirt pocket, and with a pat said, "You better keep this for now. Come on; let's get you out of here."

I wanted to tell him I intended to return it all along, but how? How could I have told him that after my first visits to that house, the dread I experienced whenever I approached as I had so many afternoons, grew disproportionately until I was no longer able to cross the street, as if I had become an immoveable object.

Soon as we were out of the district and had come to an avenue busy with traffic—I never knew how relieved I could be to once again hear the sound of traffic—and stopped at a neighborhood bakery.

We took a booth, and Reynold ordered an exotic tea and when it was served, through the curling steam he said, "You need a safe place to stay."

What he had in mind would have been unimaginable without him. It wasn't until we had gone some distance and came within a few blocks of 7th Street and Spring Garden did I realize we were headed for the house. I stopped cold, refusing to go on.

"You can't remain where you've been staying," he repeated with some sympathy. "Trust me. You can trust me, you know," and led me on, until we came to the door with its oversized metal knocker.

We stood before the invisible thing I had fought so hard to avoid, knowing if I did not submit to its will I would be left to endure indefinitely, a state of fear and confusion. This force that I could not explain, had been pulling me its way step by step all along. It was clear that I had to surrender to its compelling power no matter what my senses were telling me.

Reynold's presence—he had entered first then held the door open for me—made the experience less dreadful than I imagined. He greeted another curator at the reception desk, exchanged a few words with him that I could not hear and at once I realized he was one of Reynold's companions who chased my attackers earlier, I wanted to express my gratitude but before I could speak, Reynold took my arm and ushered me away.

"Did they catch them?" I asked.

"Almost," Reynold said, "They got a good look at them. We know who they are now," and showed me to the reading room. He shut the door then put my pack in a closet from which he removed a heavy quilt. This he shook over a sofa covered in damask; an arabesque pattern woven in gold fabric raised on a red background and said, "You should be comfortable here," and explained the place was reconstructed from what Poe himself thought such a room might look like, furnished with "rich crimson" drapes that complemented the carpet, "the soul of the apartment," a white marble, octagon-shaped table, fluted moldings and other appointments one might find in a well-designed reception and sitting chamber of the 1840s. "We're quite proud of this area, you know. It adds to the site. Poe would have been honored, don't you think? Everything is as he would have wanted it, exactly as described in one of his essays. As for the rest of the structure, the main house as you soon will see, has been deliberately maintained in a state of what conservationists call "arrested decay." It is best kept that way. Now," he turned to me, "You may come and go as you please, though I'd make myself scarce during those days when we're open to tourists, if I were you. Use my key to let yourself in. I must leave now."

Before I could ask him when I might see him again, he was gone. I went to the outer reception area and found it empty; the desk did not have its familiar attendant. The place seemed vacant. I returned to the room and sat on the edge of that ornate sofa trying to calm my apprehensions. The longer I remained, the more I became at ease. It seemed natural, and if I were anywhere else I might find this astonishing, but here, it was no longer questioned, as if my growing comfort with the surroundings I once feared was a natural result of having submitted my will. Perhaps this was a reward of some kind issued from an unknown source.

The source became apparent soon enough.

Evening descended. The place was silent. Still. The clicking of an antique clock could be heard and that was all. I laid back on the couch and no sooner had I done this, I began to drift off, and woke to what? A command? It was no less than this. Had I slept a few minutes, or a few hours? Stepping into the hallway I approached the parlor and ascended a flight of stairs to the second floor. I say ascended because it was exactly that. I did not feel the boards beneath my feet, or the effort of climbing stairs. Instead, it was if my body itself glided upward until I reached the study. It was pitch black and I stared into that blackness without emotion or thought. It was as if I was waiting for something. Slowly the moon rose and its bluish-white light came through the west window, the window where the night bird, Poe's raven once tapped on the glass with his message, and the room was suffused with a dull glow.

In this half-light I saw the empty fireplace, and the planking near the hearth where Poe's desk once stood, and then I saw it—the figure in the corner of the room. It had been there observing me since I entered. Not only could I see a human form, but the features were well defined. There he stood, arms crossed, an odd smile on his lips as if he were examining me, seeing if he found me acceptable. His embroidered vest was clear, even the pattern of the silk stitching, a glossy pale beige on ivory-white brocade, and his eyes were dark gray, almost slate. His fingernails were bitten down, but not badly, enough to notice, and he seemed rather rigid in a black frock coat and the muslin stock wound about his neck. The shape itself was like a hologram I had so often seen in laboratory settings. I had the sensation that if I touched that image I could easily pass my hand through the form. As much as I imagined doing this, I prevented myself from moving so much as an inch, fascinated by the experience itself, and fearful of what might be the consequences of such an act.

Soon as the thought passed through my mind, the image smiled— it was the kind of smile given to assure another—then he simply vanished. I stepped over to the corner it occupied and put out my hand only to touch nothing but empty space.

Poe had not only shown himself to me that night, but when I passed through the parlor, it was no longer empty. His family was there. The walls were no longer slick with worn layers of wallpaper, but were colored and decorative. A double-burner Argand lamp gave a soft glow to the surroundings, and Sissy sat near the window with her cat on her lap. A candle in a pewter tray burned on the window sill, placed there by Muddy soon as Sissy had lit it. Her mother had a dread fear of fire, and an open flame was not permitted near the furnishings. Its heat melted the frost on the window into an oval and in it, I could see the reflection of Virginia Clemm Poe, her face framed in frost. She held a little embroidered cloth in her hand which she raised to her lips occasionally.

Muddy seemed occupied, arranging bric-a-brac, all the while chatting rapidly to herself—what I could not hear—then left for the kitchen. It was then I turned away, leaving Sissy staring out the window, gently stroking Catarina curled on her lap.

*   *   *

The next morning I greeted Reynold as he was hurrying up the walk. I had gone outside to meet him, thinking we could talk before he checked in for work.

I spoke rapidly, relaying the incidents of the previous night, and my account was punctuated with questions: how could this have occurred? Why had I seen the image of man dead for more than 160 years? Was it simply an act of imagination, some hallucinogenic oddity?

Raynold stopped. His breath circled above him into the cold air as he spoke, "Are you sure?" he asked.

"Yes. I am certain of it. It was him."

"Was the experience upsetting in any way?"

"Upsetting? Not in the least. In fact, I find myself strangely fascinated by the prospect."

"Good," he said. "I hoped you would be."

"Yes, but this doesn't explain what I observed."

"No, but it seems you've been given an introduction. The fact you were permitted to see his family in his home is something of a compliment. You passed."

"Passed?"

"Yes, you passed his scrutiny. He shared with you images of his family. That alone should be enough to convince you of his interest."

Before I could inquire further, he took me by my elbow and led me up the stairs. "Perkins has something of importance. I want you to see it."

Perkins—one of the associates who chased my attackers—was at his station. Reynold led me to his desk and asked if he would show us the "find."

And with that, from under the reception table he removed that white rod that had been placed across my throat, and set it on his desktop.

"One of your assailants couldn't manage climbing over a wall and keeping this with him at the same time," Perkins said.

Reynold examined it from every angle. It was about four feet in length, with a little crook at one end. "This is hardly a walking stick," Reynold said, "far too thin, and the grip seems more for ornamental value, than for its function."

It was completely white just as I remembered it, but on inspection, it had a high luster. "It looks like ivory," I offered.

"Walrus tusk," Reynold said. He turned it over, and inside the crook, underneath its curve was the carving of some creature.

"Octopus," Reynold said, and pointed it out to me. The head was bulbous, overdrawn, and the tentacles, extremely large and wild.

"What you are looking at is a Maker's Mark," he said. "I suspect this item was made by a sea-faring man, an illiterate no doubt, though an accomplished craftsman."

"Because there is no signature . . ."

"Exactly. There's not even an initial as one might expect to find on an item like this, usually stylized. But here you have simply this . . . this caricature of a sea monster."

"But what about the scrimshaw?" I asked, referring to the symbols carved along its side.

"This is not scrimshaw," he corrected, "rather a chain of ideographs. It couldn't be anything else. Quite elaborate at that."

There was the motif of what appeared to be a star followed by a line to cross, again a line to a horizontal figure 8, then to the upper part of a half disc, another line to a teardrop symbol, and so on, the pattern repeated throughout both sides of the cane.

Perkins spoke up: "The men who meant you harm belong to a gang—the Skinners—but these are not their signs. Perhaps their canes were stolen."

"Possibly," Reynold replied. "Or maybe they were acquired in some other way. At least we have the identity of the culprits."

"Yes," Perkins agreed, "we do have that. The perpetrators most often work in tandem—a duo—petty thievery for the most part. From the descriptions given the police, we suspect they are Cobb and Dilly. They may be related, possibly brothers."

Reynold returned to the artifact. "These symbols suggest a code of some kind. Perhaps it is the signature of some union. No, this is no walking stick, though it might pass for one at a glance given by a common observer. Maybe it has a ceremonial use. However, in your case," he said looking at me, "it was a weapon."

On close inspection it appeared too elaborate, artistic, even dignified, to be an agent of violence. It looked as though its maker had other reasons for its design.

"We'll have it checked out by the police cryptologist," Reynold nodded to Perkins who secured the evidence under his desk.

"The owner will want it back. I'm sure of that," Reynold smiled with confidence. "It is too valuable a thing, certainly for a common street criminal. Besides, I suspect its importance goes beyond its material value. We'll find out one way or another." He paused a moment, looked at Perkins, and said, "I've seen these symbols before . . . somewhere."

Reynold wanted to return to the scene of the confrontation and asked me to join him, but soon as we were outside, I was aware of the same sensation I had experienced the night before when ascending the stairs. We did not take a step, instead we actually drifted, and as we progressed, moving forward always over the pavement, the atmosphere took on a peculiar quality.

The air was motionless, the sky muted with a dull gray overcast as if we were in an infinite dome in which there was no horizon, or sense of nature in any form. We soon arrived at the site of the abandoned warehouse where I had stayed. Reynold examined the graffiti about the building. Among the exaggerated images, gang tags, cartoon-like letters, there was a singular band, barely legible, faded with age, but with the same symbols that were carved into the cane recovered by Perkins in his chase.

"There," Reynold said, "this is where I recall first seeing the markings."

"The criminals must be linked to this place then," I said.

"That would be my guess, but how or why remains to be seen," and with that we began our journey once again. I expected a return to Spring Garden House, but that was not Reynold's intention.

"You asked me about your experiences last night. Let me explain what actually occurred," he said as we continued onward, turning down an avenue that was unfamiliar, and as gloomy as any I've ever seen.

"What you observed was not a dream. What you saw was Poe's astral self, his other. It was an eidolon." He paused for my reaction.

"How could that be?" I asked.

"We are two selves—the material and the nonmaterial; the self of this world, and the other self, the eternal. Like many before him, Poe assumed his eidolon at death, returning to his home during this period to do what he failed to do while he was here; to establish the great ambition of his life, his beloved magazine, *The Stylus,* and to find a cure for his wife's deadly condition, something he had not done during his lifetime, and for which he held himself personally responsible. This is what has driven his return."

He explained that an eidolon—one's astral other—may occur during life which, Reynold noted, was what I had been experiencing. "You are in good company, Dorn, and share a distinction common to poets and presidents—from Donne and Shelley, to Lincoln—history has recorded these instances with unusual interest and in uncommon detail.

Also, an eidolon may form at death, Reynold went on, when one passes from an incomplete life, a life left undone, and assumes an astral self from "sheer, incessant longing."

"And you," I asked, "what are *you* then?"

The question remained unanswered, for before us was a sight so ghastly that it silenced all thought other than attention to itself.

Each side of the street was lined with nondescript buildings, possibly residences of some kind set back some distance, but it was so dark that nearly everything was obscured.

Here were lines of gray faces together as if tiered, from porch to curb, rows upon rows of daunted figures, their countenances, ashen and bewildered. No sound could be heard, but if sound were possible, it would only be the sound of human moaning and sorrow.

Some sat, their knees drawn to their chins, other huddled in close groups. They were packed together on both sides of the street staring emptily as Reynold and I slowly passed them by, keeping to the center of the avenue. There were old men in tattered clothing, possibly bygone veterans of old soldiers' homes, a few with what appeared to be service medals on their lapels, but these were tarnished so much so they were indistinct, like brass smudges. Others gaped into nothingness; women, old and young, made oppressive by their condition, as if they had been factory workers, seamstresses, domestics, or toilers of the field, who had lived lives of exhaustion. All, everyone, man and boy, woman and child, stared blankly, open-mouthed.

We stopped. "Dorn—what you see around you—are the dead. They died without passion. They have no place in Eidolona. They have nothing to pursue, nothing to correct, nothing to achieve. They died empty, and so here they stay. This street—The Street of the Dreamless Dead—goes on for miles. Some claim it has no end."

"Is there no hope?" I asked. "Surely there must be . . ."

"None," was Reynold's reply. "They will remain here forever. They must. It is their fate. They abandoned themselves in life and there is no return for them. This is the only world they will ever know. You will not find those who pursued an unfulfilled purpose with passion among them. They are without a cause; you will not find the likes of Poe here, or anyone else who died with an unfulfilled pursuit that possessed mind and heart.

We turned off the avenue at the next corner and into a swift breeze, leaving the eternally homeless behind, and within minutes we were at the door of our destination.

It was the building that housed the tavern I knew as Eulogy, but it was in another time—the customers wore the apparel of Poe's day—and we ascended the stairs to a loft with a central table about which a few men had gathered while others sat on a bench off to the side.

"They meet here," Reynold said of the investors, "to decide on the great venture of Poe's career—what he longed for most and what would make his life, and those of his loved ones sustainable, even successful. Poe went from one publication to another, and each profited from his writings and his name. Each increased its circulation significantly while Poe's compensation was a fraction of what he should have received.

When he returned after his death to set matters straight, Griswold was waiting. Griswold, jealous of Poe in life, vilifying him in death, his eternal nemesis. He went directly to Poe before Poe contacted anyone, and confirmed he was re-assembling the original backers, now willing to fund *The Stylus*, but of course, there were conditions. Poe was not informed of the meeting and had no opportunity to address the assembly, or speak on his own behalf."

Among them, a few stood out: I recognized them from my readings and the daguerreotypes I found in Alana's books. I immediately noticed George Rex Graham, portly and good-natured; in deportment and dress clearly a man of substance and gentle authority who had once promised Poe financial support for his new venture when he worked for him as editor of *Graham's Magazine*.

Thomas Holly Chivers was unmistakable with his looming forehand and his hair flattened on either side almost touching his shoulders. He sat grim, taking in the ongoing discussion as if silently assessing the whole business.

I did not recognize Thomas Clarke, and Reynold had to point him out to me. "Clarke," he noted, "was one of the principal sponsors of Poe's project, and publisher of Philadelphia's *Saturday Museum* who withdrew his support in 1843, having trouble with his own magazine, and because he had been informed that Poe was not considered reliable."

It was a new beginning, but one that required certain understandings.

Among the understandings were the following: that the management of *The Stylus* could not be entrusted to Poe alone. Griswold assured the financiers that a profitable publication could only be achieved under his management—Poe would be unreliable—and Poe must agree to participate with an equal share in all editorial functions with the exception of actually running the operation, however he would be cited as 'co-publisher' and could expect to receive profits far exceeding anything he had earned in the past. It would be with this agreement that Poe could have his second chance.

Another consideration included a monthly column selected by Griswold alone, and featuring the opinions of 'Arcton,' who had founded a society and wished to proselytize his vision of a utopian community, and was willing to pay "a sum to great too be ignored," for the privilege.

"After Griswold convinced the investors of the necessity of his provisions which would ensure the monetary health, indeed the prosperity, of the enterprise, he met with Poe."

The room was suddenly empty of those who formerly occupied it, and there were two figures at that table, sitting across from one another, Rufus Griswold and Edgar Allan Poe.

Griswold did his best to explain the proposition to Poe in the most positive terms, and with as much pleasantness as possible.

The terms were unacceptable. Poe objected to pecuniary restrictions placed upon him, his role as co-publisher, and his limited rights to opinion pieces.

"As for Arcton and other shaman of his ilk, *The Stylus* is not for them," Poe said, reminding Griswold that the venture required a literature worthy of critical praise; writing of the first order that would entertain and illuminate, requiring the finest plates and illustrations, using English milled paper, a publication that could not be found for its "quality of thought, and superior intellectual character anywhere in the civilized world.'"

Griswold tried to reason with him, explaining the grandness of the opportunity, a one-time offer, and emphasized the trust his benefactors had placed in his judgment.

He assured him the conditions were not negotiable. Poe appeared nervous from the onset of the discussion, but now turned quickly into a state of outrage.

He pushed his chair away from the table and stood. "This is my enterprise and will rise or fall on *my* name only, and it does not exist so that we should coin our minds to silver."

As he left the meeting, the room went dark, and the next moment, Reynold and I were downstairs at our own table by a window looking out onto Chestnut Street.

The place was bustling with the lunch crowd; patrons in modern-day dress. When Reynold motioned to a server, Marcel appeared at once with that pale complexion, and a spritely bearing; all enthusiasm and nervousness at the same time. Of course, Reynold knew him, just like he seemed to know everyone in Philadelphia. He did not hesitate to order Scaldis—I recall exactly—because it was much too strong for me, and he joked that what he had to tell me "might require stronger fortification." Instead, I deferred to Marcel once again, and from among the several brews, including his own beloved Orval, I chose Bornem, named after a Belgian abbey, and Marcel said, "where this beer is the mainstay through the forty days of Lent. It has all the nutrients necessary for the monks who fast and go without food during this period every year." He seemed satisfied with his anecdote, and added, "You won't be disappointed."

"And now," I said to Reynold, "what happens to Poe? Isn't he trapped by his own ambitions? Will he not yield on a single point on the production of *The Stylus*?"

"It doesn't seem he will," Reynold affirmed. "After the meeting you just witnessed, Poe could not be found for several days. Eventually, Griswold paid a visit to his home, still firm in his proposal, but knowing also that the magazine could not gain a substantial readership without Poe's name attached, found him in a distressed state, unable to discuss plans for the periodical. In time, when the insults had dulled, and when he came around to accepting the fact that Griswold had outdone him by getting the backers to trust him more than Poe, he called out to his old friend, Lippard—"

"What do you mean," I interrupted, "when you say he 'called out?'"

"It's an expression unique to the state of the eidolon. An astral form may beckon another, or, as in your own case, a living human being. When Poe realized he had been usurped by Griswold, and once he emerged from the despair of the blow given him, he called out for his dear friend, George Lippard, that is, he concentrated his astral energies to occasion his return."

From my reading, I recalled he was a gothic writer too, a social activist, and established a workers' union. Poe saw him last, a few months before his death. "They were like brothers."

"Exactly," Reynold said. "When Poe called out, Lippard came at once. But why should I explain what happened, when you can just as easily see for yourself? I want you to take a little journey, this time without me."

I had faith in his confidence without knowing why, and I was struck with the prospect that it was possible for me to explore Eidolana on my own. Reynold held the door for me, gave me a pat on the back, and soon as I stepped out of Eulogy, I stepped into sudden darkness—what I thought was Chestnut Street only minutes before—and found myself standing instead on a hard surface, hard as any pavement, but thinly covered with moss, not enough to cushion the underlying piece of granite along the banks of a creek, and once I adjusted myself to the scene, accepted it, and did not struggle within my own mind on the sudden change of location, or try to turn back, nothing less than a new world disclosed itself.

I knew I was on the banks of the Wissahickon if only from those descriptions I had read, a nature park for Philadelphians of the period, but still retaining its secrets and woody recesses and its mystery. There was the soft murmur of waterfalls in the distance; white oaks, poplars, some scattered cedars, and among these, the distinct presence of people or animals were present, though nothing was yet visible, and everything was sensed. It was if I was in some grand attic-museum, of a size too great to calculate; dimensions too vast for measure.

The foliage, beginning at the water's edge, moved up the sides of the banks. It was dense; the leaves of the oaks were silver and gold, as if beaten to the thinnest of metals, and clicked against themselves lazily as if from a slight breeze, but there was no noticeable movement, not the subtlest waft. It did not seem to be autumn, although there was warmth to the air suggestive of Indian summer. It was then I recalled Reynold's remarks about such places, this nether world of the eidolon, part history, part fancy, neither day or night, winter or summer, wet or dry, the realm of the living dead, and those who have voyaged to meet them. The terrain, the atmosphere, even objects, took on the prospects of their human residents as if in sympathy with their states, their longings, even to reflecting the very *tone* and sentiment of their occupants. This was apparent in the aspects of the sky, which on this occasion looked like a giant dome of dull pearl mixed with splotches of muted gray. Every plant, every branch and shrub, every earthly composition gave itself to the sentiments of the participants of the scene, as if they understood their visitors and their pursuits, and commiserated with them and their cause, whatever it might be.

As I was taken up with this place, wondering how nature could correspond to the situation of its human company—or was this only an illusion within myself and part of no other thing?—or how it could exhibit such seeming empathy, there appeared two men who emerged from a forested area on a foot path under a jagged, rocky promontory with sides of flat gray slate. Later I would learn that this was the site where Poe saw the great elk in his essay on the Wissahickon, and where Lippard, after Poe's death, married in Indian ceremonial dress under a full moon.

One placed his hand on the shoulder of his companion, and his companion did likewise. They remained this way for a long while, enough for me to approach within a few yards. So engrossed were they in their discussion, neither noticed me, or if they had, I was of no concern to them. They continued on, engaged in a subject of what I judged to be of importance. There was no mistaking the fact that it was Poe himself, and the other, whose dark complexion and shoulder-length hair, his sharp features, a stature setting himself apart from other men, as much as his admiration for the elusive figures who once inhabited these woods; the mystic order of German pietists, or before them, the Lenape, whom he considered his distant Indian brothers, had to be none other than George Lippard.

It was as if there was, in the making, an understanding between the two men, a bond that could not be broken.

Once they concluded, and had walked together down that trail that would take them back to the city, I sensed another presence, and turned. I was face-to-face with Reynold. The light had gone out of the sky, and I could no longer see my surroundings.

Reynold asked about my experience. I agreed it was a rare opportunity, but unfortunately, I was not clear about their conversation, perhaps because I had not come close enough, or maybe because they were speaking in whispers.

"On some occasions the speech of eidolons is clear, on other occasions, this is not the case. With time you will be able to understand an eidolon's thoughts and intents without speech. It will be automatic. You'll see."

Reynold said that Lippard, hearing of Poe's plight, had returned with a small fortune from the sales of a novel that had struck the heart-cords of workers and advocates of social justice throughout the land. Now he was in a position to help his friend as in no other time or circumstance. Lippard would furnish a list of potential subscribers from a friend at *The Spirit of The Times*—pirated for a price— and another directory of customers from the defunct *Port Folio*. The two sources combined, would yield a first year's circulation of no less than 7,000 readers, at a household rate of five dollars per annum. With Poe as publisher and Lippard as contributing editor, the magazine could expect to climb to 50,000 subscribers in a short period of time, rivaling the most widely read periodicals, including *Graham's Magazine.*

"It was a windfall for Poe. It came when he thought all was lost, and renewed his spirits," Reynold continued, "but when Lippard later showed up at his bank to transfer the necessary funds, the bank manager took him into his office and begged for a delay. It seemed the amount would deplete his cash reserve below the level acceptable by the banking federation, and if Lippard could only wait a day or two, it would all be resolved. Lippard—compassionate by nature—and understanding the circumstances such a large transfer might create, agreed to the delay. After all, he reasoned, a day or two was not so long to wait for such a sum.

After he left the bank, he stopped by the Temple of Art tavern to meet with the journalist who had procured the subscriber lists. According to those present, they left together, and both were in good spirits. The owner of the bar who was on the premises that evening, claimed they both seemed congenial, but neither has been seen since. It's as if they vanished.

The district warden organized a manhunt, but nothing has turned up so far. They are following every possible lead—co-workers at *The Spirit of The Times*, Lippard's family and friends, and the journalist's relatives, as well."

I had other questions, but Reynold waved them off saying he was late for his rehearsal. He was a Mummer, the captain of a brigade no less, and New Year's Day would be soon upon them, and he had to attend to last minute preparations for the parade. His division was "The Fancies," a color-dress guard of sorts, marchers and mimes, "in fact," he said, "Perkins and some of the other boys are in my brigade," By 'other boys' I assume he meant some of the National Park Service employees with whom he worked. He described 'Mummery' as "a necessary distraction. It helps me keep things in balance, as one might seek recreational activities, or a favorite sport. Besides the camaraderie, it puts me in touch with the local goings on, keeps me up to date."

We parted then, Reynold went on to his rehearsal, and I returned to the Spring Garden House. The place was closed, locked up, and I was stunned to learn it was now nearing midnight. I do not know where I had been detained, or if the events at Eulogy and the Wissahickon had distorted my sense of time. Once among eidolons, time and place had a wild logic of their own, misshapen to any former reference I may have held. Perhaps the journey itself consumed the sense of temporal passage, shortening it, or prolonging it, in accord with equations beyond earthly understanding.

I entered using Reynold's key, went directly to the reading room, and put myself to bed in that crimson arabesque sofa, under the comforter Reynold provided.

*   *   *

After all the excitement that night, I fell to sleep immediately, into a kind of stupor and only came around hours later when I heard a commotion in the other room.

It was Reynold, opening up the place. He had arrived for his shift. The light was just coming in the windows and it was early, even for him.

"Dorn?" he said standing outside the reading room in his Mummer's costume, with those exaggerated neon-colored feathers in his headband, still in make-up, he must have come directly from the station where he was working with his division, putting the final touches on the routines for the upcoming yearly parade.

"I think you should see this," he said. "Come around to the back".

By the time I straightened up the sofa, folded and stored away the blanket, and joined him at the rear of the house, he had already changed into his government uniform, the olive-green pants and jacket of the National Park Service.

The body lay in a heap on the wooden storm cellar door.

It was that of a young female. She wore a tight-bodiced chemise with puffed sleeves. A woolen shawl lay in a pile. Her hair was dull blond, fine as it was profuse, tied in a bun with a blue ribbon.

Raynold stood over the body. "I was afraid it would come to something like this." A thin necklace of red, like a ruby choker, ran under her chin. Raynold squatted down to examine it without touching the corpse. The head itself was askew, oddly twisted. Raynold removed something that had been tucked in her waist scarf, which matched the material of the ribbon in her hair. He carefully unfolded it, and scrawled in crude pencil was the following:

> *A bright loss, more or less,*
> *But consider this,*
> *With Pride there is such pain,*
> *Eternal pain & anguish,*
> *More with less, & always this—*
> *Love, will any love remain?*

He took the note. "This should interest the authorities."

"Shouldn't you tell him first?" I asked.

"Him?"

"Yes, you know, Poe. Shouldn't you be telling Poe," I heard my voice rise.

"He already knows." Reynold looked up at me, and for a moment appeared to study me somehow, as if something was not understood.

As much as I wanted an explanation then and there, I knew the house would be soon overrun with police.

I returned to the reading room to get my backpack and the few necessities it contained, so I would not be there when they arrived, and no one would know I spent the night. I wanted to give my farewell to Reynold, but when I came around to the side of the house, expecting to find him still with the body, he was not there. And the corpse, the beautiful young woman who lay crumpled on the slanting storm cellar doors only moments before, was gone.

*   *   *

I did not return to the house for some time, assuming the site was overrun with watchmen and constables, even the district warden, a fellow named McGurdy, who called himself "The Investigator," and who acquired a reputation for determination and did not compromise the obedience he required of his subordinates.

The problem with McGurdy was his record. By any account it was less than adequate. For every ten crimes, there was one apprehension. But nothing dissuaded him from his diligence. He remained certain of his prowess while others questioned whether he should be kept in office at all. He would have been removed years ago, but he was by marriage related to the aging Mayor who, whenever his detractors would come forth, argued for his position, and his competence. McGurdy had yet to come up with any leads that would help find Lippard, or the journalist he had befriended for a price. He did prove useful in using Perkins' description of my assailants, tying them to the criminal records of some inhabitants of the dubious area known as "Gray's Ferry," in south Philadelphia, otherwise known as "The Forgotten Bottom," where their mother, a figure well-known to the under culture, a fortune teller and palmist, made her home. A place I never thought I would visit, but would soon enough.

Reynold arranged to meet me at his favorite bakery. He seemed to treasure the tea served there. "I can't seem to find it anywhere else," he said, bringing up the aroma with his hand. He closed his eyes to savor the steam. "It's Ti Kwan Yin, an Oolong, from the province of Fujian. I've never been there myself—southeast coast of China—although I'd very much like to travel there someday. Care for some?"

"No, not at the moment, thank you. I'm more concerned about the girl—"

"It goes well with scones, of all things."

A scone arrived with a side of warm honey. Raynold insisted on it, "to complement the tea, of course," he smiled. "Confections are one of my weaknesses. See," he said, taking the little crystal dipper from the cruet, "you drizzle it over the scone." He worked a line, zigzagging it over the pastry, until he was satisfied with the design, let it rest to absorb into the flakey surface, then cut into it with his fork.

I wanted to know about the girl.

"We'll get to that soon enough. Do you intend on attending the Mummer's Parade? I hope so. It's quite the event."

"I'm sure it is, but I've not made plans. What about the victim?" I persisted.

"Yes, yes. Well, here it is: her name is Eliza White. Sound familiar?"

"One of Poe's acquaintances, wasn't she? The daughter of a publisher, I believe. He met her before he married Virginia."

"Yes, and she was more than an acquaintance. Eliza White was the daughter of the publisher of *The Southern Messenger*, Thomas Willis White. She was eighteen when Poe first met her. Uncommonly attractive. Well, you've seen her, regrettably. Her role in Poe's life, whether she knew it or not, was a catalyst."

"How do you mean?"

"Poe's interest in her bloomed into a rumor of romance in a matter of weeks, and news of it worked its way back to Maria Clemm, and she, fearing she might lose Poe, had written to him suggesting she—and her daughter, Virginia—might move in with a prosperous cousin, Neilson Poe, who, she claimed, was willing to give Virginia the kind of upbringing she deserved; provide her with an affluent home, access to private tutors, entrées to the finest cultural events, and so on. It's not known if she had any serious intention of actually taking Sissy to live with Neilson, nonetheless, she certainly convinced Poe that she was inclined to accept, for her daughter's sake if nothing else, to improve her life so Virginia would not be subject to the hardships she had endured herself.

Poe wrote a heart-breaking appeal to Maria—and Virginia—to remain together as a family, and to refuse Neilson's proposal. To appreciate Poe's desperation, we must understand he had not only lost his own family—his parents—when he was an infant, but lost his second family as well. Only a year before, John Allan died, the man who raised him—and later disowned him—as well as his wife, Frances, who was Poe's surrogate mother.

In any case, Poe returned within a few months and married Virginia, and it was because of Eliza, and of course, Maria's threat of taking Virginia away which would have meant another family leaving him, something he could not bear.

As for Poe's unusual regard for the women in his life, including Eliza, I believe Alana could describe that phenomenon better than I."

"Alana?" I asked. "You've heard from her?"

"We keep in touch. In fact, if you like, she can give you her perspective on the matter."

"She's here?" I asked.

"Let me contact her. Then I'll inform you. Agreed?"

I nodded.

"In the pantheon of Poe's women, Eliza White was not an insignificant figure; Poe adored her in the way he adored so many other female figures in his life, but she did not have the status; did not possess the more complex and endearing sensibilities of the more influential women that you will have the opportunity of seeing this evening. When you return to the Spring Garden House it will all become apparent. We have an invitation, by Poe himself, and it's one I think we should honor."

"Yes," I agreed, stunned by the prospect.

There was a pause. Reynold drew a deep breath and became solemn. His lightheartedness that attended the beginning of our discussion was now gone. The precious leaves of Oolong, removed from the cup after a minute's steeping, which he had timed precisely, lay curled on the saucer; what they had to give, was given, and now they were useless; the plate with its few flakes of dried pastry was set aside. It was as if he had been avoiding all along the grim event he now faced.

"When the body was examined, the attending physician made some notes and passed them on to the warden's office. I've since reviewed them, with McGurdy's permission.

We know Eliza White's carotid arteries were severed by use of a garrote, but there's something else that emerged when the body was examined, something intentionally kept from Poe, for fear that if he knew, the knowledge might so discourage him that he would forsake his pursuits, or worse. The facts might so affect him as to endanger his very life.

Inspection of Eliza's body revealed horizontal welts from the back of the thighs up to the buttocks. Some had been healed over, then broken again by repeated injury. Are you familiar with the practice of caning?" Reynold asked.

"Isn't it a form of corporeal punishment? Its origins are in the east, aren't they? It's been used at various times as both a military and civil penalty." I said, offering what little I knew.

"Exactly, and used with brutal consequences. The affects of caning are painful, with scars often carried to the transgressor's grave. But perhaps more than this, they remain as a constant reminder of humiliation.

In the case of Eliza White, it is now obvious that she had received such canings on several occasions before her death. From this, we may presume she had been punished for some time prior to her demise—maybe weeks. The object of this is unclear. Perhaps it was meant to cause Poe even greater remorse."

"And all of this is an attempt to have Poe concede his stake in *The Stylus*, and accept Griswold's terms?" I asked.

"So it would seem. And if this is true, if young Eliza's murder was for this sole purpose, then there is no telling what her murderers might be capable of. McGurdy and his constables are keen on last line of the verse tucked in her waist band, 'Love, will any love remain?' and with their sentiment I must concur: it seems that other loves may be in danger of a similar fate if Poe remains determined in his convictions.

Then as if worn by the gravity of the situation, Reynold added, "I am going now for a bit of rest before this evening. I suggest you do the same."

*   *   *

Rest was impossible. My mind raced with possibilities: was Griswold, a man of undoubted deception, able to commit such a heinous act as befell Eliza White? Was he even capable of complicity in the most grievous of criminal offenses, the act of murder? And could he have been involved with Lippard's disappearance? Or that of his colleague?

Soon it was the appointed time. I knew this not by any clock, or signal, only by that unique sense of urgency I had experienced on my first night, when I ascended that staircase to the study of Edgar Poe on the second floor of the Spring Garden House.

As before, I entered in the dark and remained for some time until anyone arrived.

The first to appear was Reynold and he stood next to me, then shortly after, I could discern Poe himself, who occupied he same corner as he had before; his features, severe. He had with him what looked like a little scroll of some kind. It was tied with a ribbon, and he held it in hand against his chest.

Poe moved across the room, set the item on the mantle of the fireplace and made a sweeping motion with his arm. At this moment a circle of chairs appeared. Each was occupied by a different figure. All were dressed in black. Each held the hand of the next. It would have been a closed sphere were it not for one unoccupied seat. It was almost like a séance, or some other meditative ritual, and not a word was uttered.

Reynold shifted his attention from one woman to the next. Their heads were bowed in mourning. He whispered, "These are the others, the 'loves,' one would imagine referenced in the note left on Eliza's body. The empty chair symbolizes her absence from her sisters in the service of saving Poe from further torment, and themselves from a similar fate. They have so gathered themselves together at Poe's behest, placing aside whatever differences they may have had in life. He wants us to see them for ourselves, in an intimate setting; more precisely, he wants *you* in particular, to witness this unique group assembled here to grieve Eliza's death and to demonstrate their solidarity in their devotion to one of their own, and to Poe as well."

Reynold went around the circle, making remarks about each: there was Sarah Helen Whitman, a psychic who believed she was spiritually connected to Poe as they shared the same birth date. Whitman believed she could speak to the dead, and gave weekly séances. She was subtle yet dramatic, wearing a miniature wooden coffin around her neck, and claimed the ether she took, soaking it in her handkerchief, was for a heart condition. Poe and Whitman were once engaged, less than a year before his death, but she broke if off because he was seeing another woman, and Whitman heard it rumored that Poe had been observed at the bar of a local hotel. She remained a loyal supporter of Poe however, publishing a book, *Edgar Allan Poe and His Critics* in his defense, aimed at the injurious remarks penned by Griswold after Poe's death.

Seated beside her was Marie Louise Shew, married to a physician when she first met Poe in New York City during the harsh winter of 1837 when he had gone to public dispensary for treatment for a persistent head cold. Later, in Fordham, she nursed Virginia, and after her death, consoled Poe. He once complained to her of headaches that were exacerbated by the tolling of church bells. He was more disconsolate because he had wanted to write a poem for the past several days, but lacked the necessary inspiration.

Marie Louise too, was a catalyst. On that evening, when Poe was distraught over his condition, she wrote on a slip of paper, "The bells, the little silver bells," the beginning of one of the most metrically perfect poems ever written. The two of them made a game of it, and Poe sketched out several stanzas with her encouragement, with "The Bells" as its title.

There were others: Annie Richmond, Sarah Elmira Royster—Poe's first—and last—love; Francis Sargent Osgood, a popular nineteenth-century poet who carried on with Poe a public exchange of romantic poems that suggested an affair which may have led to the birth of a child, Fanny Fay, who died in infancy. This relationship caused a scandal from which Poe never recovered. It followed him to his grave. Of course, included in the gathering was Rosalie, Poe's sister, who fawned over him ceaselessly, and she sat next to Maria and Virginia.

Each woman had her own story, her own unique relationship with Poe that Reynold seemed to know in specific detail, and each, he said, "could very well be the next victim, and they know all it."

With a gesture of Poe's hand, the distinguished assembly disappeared. Reynold was no longer by my side. I was alone. Poe lifted the small scroll from the mantle and held it out to me. I knew I was to take it from him, and even if I could refuse, I would never have done so; the prospect of accepting a material object from him—it could have been any anything—was simply too great a temptation. Simultaneously, I understood that accepting it meant accepting more than the thing itself. Even though I knew this, knew the consequences might not be as I wished, my senses seemed excited by the gesture. I held out my hand. As soon as the rolled paper was in my palm, Poe was gone.

The sense of knowing generally what Poe wanted was strong, but trying to understand his exact intentions, that was another matter.

"One that should become resolved with time," Reynold said when I returned to the reading room downstairs.

I removed the thin ribbon from the roll; it was the same color of blue that Eliza had worn when her body was discovered. The paper was a similar color, but not as distinct. The manuscript itself consisted of four or five pages, perhaps five by seven inches, and bore Poe's characteristic handwriting, each letter shaped in proportion to others in the word, and the words to the sentences, and the sentences to the page. It was as if he had written the manuscript to mathematical scale. Whatever emotion and energy was contained in those words, were controlled in those painfully concentrated, precise letters.

Reynold stood over my shoulder and looked at the manuscript. "Ah, it's a mythic prophecy*" he said. "It is original—written for a specific purpose. It's for you."

"Me? Why me?"

"It's an exchange, something for you to take back to the world, *your* world, when this business of *The Stylus* has been settled—and the murder of this helpless innocent—so others may know of Poe's ongoing plight, but above all, the truth of astral existence.

This manuscript is unknown in Poe's *oeuvre*, he continued. No doubt it will be inspected, probed, criticized, but in the end, I suspect in a matter of a few short months, it will emerge as one of the great literary discoveries of the century, and indisputable proof of Poe's astral presence. People will believe you, influential people. It is important that others know there is such a region as this, where forms exist, more than phantoms, or fragments of imagination, where reanimation of images that are more than images, acting out of their own volition to attain goals that eluded them in their earthly existence.

In his lifetime, Poe tried again and again to disclose the world of the eidolon, and now he has found someone who can take his message back into the world, so that others may know of its reality; that there is a life within our lives that offers the hope of renewed creation."

---

* The mythic prophecy has been included in its entirety at the conclusion of this narrative.

I had become the trustee of a dead man who placed in my care an item exceeding any material worth, no matter how extravagant, which was evidence of a phenomenon that would otherwise be dismissed as lunacy by any rational person.

I set the manuscript on the table, as if to separate myself from it. Reynold was aware of my hesitation, I knew. I could feel it.

"You've already accepted the exchange," he reminded me. "You shouldn't have any trouble with your credibility. I should think a couple of well-placed journal articles would start things rolling. I'm sure you will find an appropriate set of scientific explanations for the images that populate the realm of the eidolon. After all, you are well known in this field, isn't that true?"

"Yes, but I may not be able to convince others as easily as you might think," I said.

"However, your experience here, among the spectral beings of Poe's continuing life, would itself create enough interest that would lead to an acceptance of an astral existence," Reynold said sternly.

"My colleagues are a skeptical lot. It would take years before we could adequately convince by scientific method . . ."

Reynold became calm, almost conciliatory, and for the first time, used my full name.

"You are at the top of your game, aren't you?" He smiled gently. Nominated last year to the American Academy of Arts and Sciences, it's youngest member no less, and the work you've done on topo-graphical magnetic resonating imagery has you up for the Kepler Award. And here you are, Dr. Dorn—Chester Faraday Dorn—" he mused, "with the opportunity of a lifetime—to return, hailed as an explorer of an unknown region, and to divulge for the first time in

history, its very nature, how it is accessed, what can—and cannot—
be done here, and you are? You are what? . . . *Reluctant?*"

"I'm trying to assess what I might actually be able to do—"

"I understand, but you are Poe's hope, and not only as an intermediary, but as someone who can explain his struggle, that he
continues to be victimized, and there is something else, something I
myself have been reluctant to reveal. You see, Poe in his life, and here
in the world you now share, is desperate to find some treatment that
will offer the hope of a cure for his beloved Virginia. Although he
continues to seek an antidote, he realized, once Eliza had died, there
must be some modern technological means of returning her to her
astral state, and called out to the modern world—"

I interrupted. "We are only now beginning to anticipate the
technology necessary for the interanimation of human holograms,"
I said. "Interference and diffraction physics place our best estimates
decades away, and the obstacles are many. It is flattering, however,
that Poe would place so much confidence in the capability of modern
science—"

"As you will see," Reynolds continued, "Poe will do anything, go
to any lengths, suffer any assault, accept any hardship, forego any
indignity to save those he loved while he lived. After all, this was his
wish when he first called out to me on his deathbed."

"There was only his physician present," I said.

"Indeed?" he smiled.

"It is what the biographers say. He did cry out for Reynolds, but
that couldn't—"

"Have been me?" he seemed amused. "*Biographers,*" he scoffed.
"What do they know? Were they there? No. Not a one."

"No one was there, no one but Dr. Moran," I said.

"Yes, his physician, Moran, a notorious fabulist. He made a life fictionalizing Poe's last days at the hospital. He went about the country giving lectures, and made things up as he went along, always embellishing the story in greater detail at every telling."

Here, Reynold's voice lowered, and he stared at the little Cherrywood table in front of him, and traced his finger in a circle on its surface, then again, retracing an imaginary form. "Oh, Poe called out to me as he was dying, as so many have through time, long before his own. No, we were not strangers. I have never been a stranger to a great spirit in need. Yes, he cried out, but he did not cry out for Reynolds the explorer, or Reynolds the creditor, or Reynolds the carpenter, but to me, Reynold, who, Poe trusted, would escort him to this parallel world of eidolons to pursue the great passions that eluded him in life."

At this moment, there was a soft knock on the door of the reading room. It was Alana, who entered briskly, as if in a hurry; giving me a peck on the cheek and a polite smile, then a token embrace for Reynold.

"I came as quickly as possible—"

"Yes, well, I want you to explain to Dorn here—"

"About the women?"

"Exactly."

She turned to me. "Maybe it might help to understand Poe's situation—why the women in his life were nearly sacred to him, certainly precious by all accounts if it's understood that since the time he was an infant, about the age of three, when his mother died, he believed, in his child's mind, she had abandoned him. Therefore, he must have done something dreadful to cause her to leave him forever, a thought that haunted him all his life; that he was guilty of some unknown act, and for the rest of his life he sought out women not only as a source of comfort and reassurance, but also to please them, as he might have pleased his own mother. In this way, odd as it might sound, he wanted to atone for a childhood crime that he never committed."

Alana had scarcely finished when we all heard a commotion coming from another part of the complex. We rushed from the reading room to the main house, and Poe's living room.

The front door was half-way open and Poe was arguing with a messenger who was trying to explain to Poe that he was only a courier in the service of the financiers who wished to invest in *The Stylus*.

Poe would have none of it and tried pushing him away from the door, when Muddy intervened and tried to reason with him. There were animated gestures; the messenger removed a large envelope from a leather bag slung over his shoulder.

"Sir," he said, "I've been told by my benefactors that this," he held out the packet, "would please the master of the house. Its terms are generous, and if he could bring himself to accept it, if not for himself, then for my sake, then I could say I had completed my task."

When Poe tried to close the door, Muddy stepped between him and the boy. "Eddie," she said to him, "Your muse is calling. Go listen," and accepted the documents, then pressed a coin into the boy's palm.

Poe refused to go upstairs to his study and stood fuming in the parlor. Muddy unfolded the contents of the packet.

"Here," she said, "these are the terms for *The Stylus*. When you have quieted down, you might want to read them."

Poe snatched the papers from Maria, and went directly to the fireplace where the last embers were slowly burning down, and tossed the contract onto the glowing coals. In moments, the folded sheets crackled, then burst into flame.

Reynold turned to me, "We should go."

I thought Alana would return with us, but she had moved over to Virginia who was on the couch, and in her hand, a lace handkerchief which she held to her mouth. Alana bent down beside her and placed her hand on the side of her face. Although there was some exchange I couldn't make out, it was clear to me Alana's was an act of consolation.

Reynold, observing me, said, "Alana is familiar with all the women who have found themselves in this difficult and compromising situation, especially Virginia."

Seeing how distraught she was, I said, "I would think Poe himself would look after her."

"Poe? Yes. He cares so much he has nearly become an invalid himself. Perhaps you should see the depths of his concern firsthand."

*   *   *

It seemed Poe had tried everything to help his wife's consumption; the cures of the day—herbs, Jew's beer, a variety of poultices, and failing to remove her from her family to a sanitarium newly opened in the mountains of the east, something he could do only if successful with *The Stylus*—but nothing seemed to work, and her condition worsened.

"Before Lippard vanished," Reynold said "—either abducted or murdered is my guess—he informed Poe of a miracle worker in a shanty town—Sister Sara—a name she's taken to protect her identity, and Poe had made the trip out to see her, and although Lippard offered his companionship, Poe refused, saying 'This is something I must see to myself.'"

"Come," Reynold said, and held out his hand which I reached

out for, but grasped nothing; turned to affirm his presence, and saw nothing.

When the rush of movement—what else could it be called?—diminished and visible forms began once again to take shape, there was Reynold, smiling, at my side, and we were moving, or more exactly, drifting easily through thickets, over rural landscapes, until we arrived at an embankment, and before us lay the fabled "Gray's Ferry," south of the city, an outcast place with hundreds of small fires dotted here and there around which small groups were huddled, the poor, the dispossessed, those the world no longer wants or needs.

Near the fires, we could see ratty tents, lean-to's, makeshift coverings of discarded planks, driftwood, anything that would offer some resistance to the elements. This was truly the "Bottoms," or as its inhabitants say, "The Forgotten Bottoms."

As we moved closer, her figure came into focus: Sister Sara sat crossed-legged on a straw mat outside a hastily-made shelter of rotting boards and old canvas. In front of her was an "all purpose," a metal drum used, in turns, for laundry, cooking, making potions, and at the moment, sending out heat from burning whatever debris had been scavenged and put there.

She was conversing with a tall, skinny fellow who stood over her in short-style top hat, frayed, like the man himself. He sported scars on his face, and when he saw Poe nearing the fire, he shuffled up the little hill to the shelter and stayed out of sight.

The woman said she had been expecting Poe all along. Somehow she knew he was distraught over his beloved wife who had been in the miracle worker's mind for some time.

The flames flickered in such a way as to illuminate her face, which seemed glossy as if she had used an oil tonic. Her hair was tangled, and she squinted when she spoke.

All the time she was conversing with Poe, she sipped from a medicine bottle half-filled with a clear liquid, and between sips, set it down on a rock that served as a crude, uneven table, on which there were several sacred objects: a leather pouch with a beaded Indian design, a tray of various herbs tied in small bundles, a pendant on a long chain, a mirror, the size of her palm, set in an oriental frame in which, it was claimed, Sister Sara could see the images that would affect one's life—past, present, and future. At one point, she offered her medicine bottle to Poe, saying it was an elixir that would help him see more clearly, but he sharply waved it off.

No sooner had he done this, Sister Sara mumbled an incantation, moving her hand above the mirror, and summoned Poe to look at what she conjured. There, reflected in the glass, was not the likeness one would expect—the image of the poet himself—but the face of his poor wife, Virginia, and thus proof of Sister Sara's magical power.

She then poked about the leather pouch, fingered through the tray of herbs, and not finding what she wanted, called back up the hill behind her, and within moments, her companion appeared. She whispered something in his ear, and from the inside of his long coat, he removed a small, folded paper envelope of the kind pharmacists used. He gave it to Sara who examined the contents, then placed it near her heart, again with inaudible incantations.

Her directions to Poe were clear: two pinches—they must be slight, no more than a few granules—of the white powder every morning at sunrise, and the same at sunset for seven days. Then Poe was to return and inform of her its effects.

Sara claimed the medicine was acquired by her companion, whom she introduced as 'Frisco Red,' a reference to his habit of travelling abroad from a port in San Francisco, and the other part of his name was acquired when living among the plains Indians for several years, and from that experience he was dubbed "Red" by his fellow whites.

She then encouraged her partner to endorse the curative powers of the powder, obtained from tribal healers in the east, a mixture of rare herbs, residue of ground white buffalo horn, and the dried leaves of a plant so rare that botanists had recorded it as extinct. 'Frisco Red gave his own testimonial: his voice gravelly, at times indistinct, he told of great plains' warriors with mortal wounds who were cured when only a few grains were placed under the tongue, and once, a chief, thought dead, was returned to life and lived into old age.

But would this do for Virginia? Virginia, laboring with the signs that foretold with near certainty, emaciation and a slow death by suffocation. Poe wanted to believe, but still remained skeptical.

Sara pointed to living proof: 'Frisco himself had survived the same scourge with the same telltale signs. He had overcome the early stages of consumption with doses of this sacred powder taken just as Sister Sara had prescribed.

But there was a price. What could Poe pay?

He reached inside his coat for his wallet, and as he did, Sara's eyes widened. He had no money himself, only that which Lippard had given him.

Sara placed the bills inside the cuff of her blouse, and shook her head from side to side. It wasn't enough. What else did Poe have?

Trade was on her mind: in exchange for the balance of the payment for the concoction, she would accept something personal from

Poe. She would accept a poem, but not any poem, not one he had written, or published, that he could jot down for her and be on his way, no, it had to be an original. One of a kind.

What then? Did she have a subject in mind? A favorite place perhaps? One that would lend itself to poetic treatment.

Sara looked up at the heavens, and spoke of beings she had never seen, but wished to see, and swore she would spend her last days pursuing, the creatures rumored to have magical powers more mysterious than her own, the legendary elves of an untold realm.

'Frisco went to the shanty and returned with a sheet of blank paper and a pencil stub. These he gave to Poe. Sister Sara furnished a flat piece of board, and Poe placed it on his lap.

He wrote quickly in the glow of firelight, crossing out a word here or there, but he finished in a matter of minutes and presented her with what she desired.

FAIRY ELVES

A Reunion

Sleeping, sleeping still with iridescent wings
With all their earthly things the elfin world brings,
    A dew-drop rain, a rain from far away, sweeping drop by drop,
Sweeping over the top, the top of the toadstool graves,
    The homes of fairy elves, of their little elfin selves,

    To wake them, to shake them, to shake their tiny wings
To flutter and mutter and fly away high
    Away from the clatter and the chatter and the toadstool graves
Far onto that holy plane of fairy flight, that has neither night nor day
    Nor dewy rain nor elfish selves or elfish pain.

Sister Sara read it, then read it again, and pressed it to her heart. She picked up the pendant from her rock table—a rough-cut piece of quartz embedded with a bit of mica—hung from a fine chain, and spun it, placing a hand over her eyes. When the charm stopped spinning, Sara looked at the amulet and said, "This has given me your true course. When you leave, and you must leave soon, you must go directly to the fondest object of your heart," then leaned forward, her face again glowing in the firelight and said firmly, "Do not delay."

The exchange concluded, Sister Sara gave Poe her blessing, and we watched as he walked away, diminished, then indistinct from the darkness itself.

Sara and 'Frisco sat a while by the fire, and I saw the light glimmer on his face, and when I looked at his neck, saw the red outline of that same bulbous-headed octopus I had seen on the ivory cane that nearly took my life, and pointed it out to Reynold, who nodded and said, "We will pass *that* bit of information on to the authorities."

When Poe had gone, Sister Sara took another sheet of paper, and jotted down the poem without reference to its author, then handed it to her companion, and said, "Here, see what the magazines are willing to give for this. But don't let it go for cheap."

"They will want to know who penned it," 'Frisco said.

"Tell them you represent the author who wishes to remain anonymous. They'll take it anon," and took the original manuscript with Poe's signature and tucked it away in a padlocked chest she kept hidden under the rug that covered the dirt floor of her shanty. Then she snapped shut the canvas flaps that served as her doors.

With the two of them out of sight, Reynold faced me. "We'll not return as we came; we'll take Poe's route back. I want to show you something."

We took the route from The Bottoms all the way back to the southern part of town, and once there, continued on until we came to a tavern.

Reynold stopped. Tiny flakes of snow were beginning to drift about us. "Before we go in, you should know that Poe had every intention of returning home to Virginia and had taken the most direct route as Sister Sara advised, however it occurred to him that he had made a pact with Lippard: that should Sister Sarah produce a magical cure-all, they would celebrate with a toast—just one— to Virginia's health. Of course, that agreement had been made in the late fall and it was now early winter and winter had come without any knowledge of Lippard's whereabouts. He had been kidnapped, or worse. Still, there was cause to celebrate new hope for Virginia, and to honor Lippard's pact—and his memory—Poe stopped at the appointed tavern exactly as he promised Lippard he would do. And he would have one drink. Just one. Then he would be on his way home to share his prize with Sissy."

Poe sat at the bar, ordered a glass of port, and as he finished it, there was a shout from the back of the room; an editor at *The Spirit of The Times* recognized him and came over with some friends. They insisted on buying him a round, after all, he had a short story coming out in *Graham's Magazine* and it was sure to be the talk of the town, and they were all so honored to be in the presence of the author . . . and of course, it could not stop there, a third round then, one for the road, and about the time finished his glass, he noticed a draft of icy air followed those who came into the tavern, and, looking out a window, saw swirls of snow descending through the night. A storm was coming in. It was time to leave.

As he stepped outside, the wind came up in gusts. It was of such strength that Poe had to hold the lapels of his coat, his arms crossed, so as to protect himself from the viciousness of the sudden change in the weather, and if he had not done this, the wind might blow the clothes off his back, and after fighting the wind for a few blocks, staggering against the growing power of the storm, he stepped into an alleyway, between two buildings.

There he gathered himself, took a deep breath, shook off the snow, straightened himself for another onslaught, preparing himself to re-enter the squall, and then, impulsively, as if he feared he had somehow lost his most precious possession, patted his pockets, and when this did not reveal the little square envelope, he dug around, and finally, deep down, he found the packet. He was touching it with his fingertips. Then it was in the palm of his hand.

At that point, instead of pushing it back down into the safety of his greatcoat, he was struck with strange doubt. He wanted to be certain he was still in possession of the rarest of medicines. He removed it, and stared at it, if only to assure himself that it was there, safe in his grasp.

Still, this was not enough. It was not enough to know that he had in his hand, for certain, this most precious antidote. What of its contents? Were the fine grains still there? What if they had somehow become dislodged from their packet?

Or maybe it was the wild storm, or the port at the tavern that caused him doubt. In any case, Poe had to be sure. Protecting the packet with the side flap of his coat, he cautiously lifted the folds of the paper. There it was, enough white powder to fill a teaspoon.

Reassured, he breathed a sigh of relief, and just at that moment, instead of closing the little envelope and returning it safely to his pocket, he looked up, suddenly alert to his surroundings. A noise startled him. Perhaps an animal—an alley rat—had knocked over a tin can that rattled down the cobblestones. It was enough to distract his attention, if just for an instant, and in that instant, the storm, as if it knew of this hidden place, turned, as errant winds often do, rushing in odd directions, and swung sharply into the alley in a chaotic burst, blowing back the side of Poe's coat used to shield the precious contents from the erratic weather, and before he could possibly understand what was happening, whirled the powder upward in a tiny spiral, then dispersed the crystals into the icy air beyond any hope of recovery.

He was left gripping the paper, void of its contents, cursing the capricious forces of the night.

*   *   *

The following days were difficult; Poe took to his room, then to his bed, then back to his room, never venturing downstairs, avoiding his family. He made no mention of the incident to Virginia or to Maria, who said she had seen him in this state before, and that he was "inconsolable."

He complained of a headache, took to bed, then later he developed a fever. He needed a sedative, something to take his temperature down. "I'm all burning up," he said to Maria, who summoned the doctor, but did not know how to pay for his services.

The physician arrived the following day prepared to treat a fever. He administered a combination of ground willow bark and meadowsweet, and advised fasting to lower the body's heat.

After Maria showed him to the door, promising to pay "on account," Sissy was in his room—against the doctor's orders—with a steaming bowl of vegetable broth made from boiled roots and vegetables from a friendly neighbor's garden, then strained. After all, he needed nourishment, and broth couldn't hurt.

When Poe continued into the next day without much reprieve, Maria summoned the physician again, who, this time, prescribed—and administered at the bedside—tincture of morphine which put Poe into a deep sleep.

The following morning I was awakened by a commotion outside the reading room, in the main lobby. There was Poe himself struggling with the door, too weak to open it, and soon Virginia and Maria joined him. Each stood on either side of him, holding one of his arms, and escorting him, despite his protests, toward the stairway, and up to his room. All the time he was mumbling about returning to Gray's Ferry, that it was "imperative" that he leave at once.

From this, I gathered he was determined to retrace his steps; visit the old witch of "The Bottoms" and to barter for another packet of magic powder for his beloved Sissy. I knew he would go, and knew as well, he was in no condition, but that he would rest and heal, if only to comfort his wife and mother, and then as of a mind with one purpose, return to his mission.

Just as the threesome disappeared up the stairs, there was the sound of the latch opening the main door, and I saw Reynold beckoning me to join him.

"We haven't much time," he said. "I managed to work in a meeting with the district warden. He just received the cryptologist's report."

"McGurdy?" I asked.

"None other."

We went immediately to the District Police Affairs Office, and were seated in an area before the registration desk, and told to wait; that Chief McGurdy would be with us presently. The brief wait would have been uneventful were it not for two officers who brought in a scruffy-looking character for booking. He gave me a furtive glance, before he was led off to a holding cell.

"Know him?" Reynold asked.

"I'm not sure, but he seems familiar."

An officer came out and led us to McGurdy's office, and there, on his desk was the ivory cane—the one that nearly took my life.

"These," he said pointing to the markings on the cane, "have been decoded." He had the cryptologist's report on a clipboard.

"Here you see the . . . the . . ." he hastily consulted the report, "the sig—sig—"

"Sigla," Reynold spoke up, helping him out.

"Um, yes, sigla, the row of signs on both sides of the shaft that mean more to the owner than one might suppose on first impression. Our cryptologist claims the two stars

on either end of the chain suggest," and here he returned to the report, "'a celestial presence that is continual, joined by the Greek cross revealing a divine equality among the symbols in eternity, expressed by the figure 8 on its side, a rising sun, which represents hope, a tear drop for suffering which is inexorable, and quite possibly necessary in some way we may not understand at the moment, and the omega symbol to say nothing is greater than this, and it is the last of all possible notions on the creed.'"

"The creed of a secret union," Reynold said.

"So it would seem," McGurdy confirmed.

That would have ended our meeting, but I asked about the district's most recent catch. "That fellow," I said, "the one that was just brought in, who is he?"

"A petty criminal," McGurdy said. "Why?"

"He seems familiar. I've seen him before." I said.

McGurdy appeared enlightened. "Let's go have a look," he said, then summoned two officers, and we all went down the hallway to the holding cell.

The man, in shabby clothing, was curled up in a corner of the cubicle.

"You," McGurdy called out, "Do you know this man?" he pointed to me.

"No, sir. Never saw 'em in all my life.

McCurdy turned to one of the booking officers. "Name?"

"Aloysius Grackle," he replied.

"Crime?"

"Trying to sell stolen goods, two counts, intermediary with intent to philander, one count. We found him loitering outside The Philadelphian. Umm," he scribbled something down, "loitering, that's another count," the officer noted.

"What were you doing at The Philadelphian?" McGurdy asked of one of the most prestigious gentlemen's clubs in the city.

"I was waiting for my master, I was."

"And who might that be?" McGurdy asked.

"A respectable citizen, who, I'm pleased to say, I am, is my employer."

"Name?" McGurdy wanted to know.

"Mr. William May. Owns The Spectacle Shoppe on 4th Street. A most respectable establishment. Started off as a lens grinder, he did, and worked his way up like we's 'posed to. Some of us, anyway. Caters only to gentry, I might add, I might."

One of the officers stepped forward and whispered something in McGurdy's ear.

"Do you know Mr. May by any other name?" McGurdy asked.

"No, sir, no not me."

"Do you know him by the name of Arcton?"

"Oh, well, let me see," he said rubbing his face as if to remember. "Maybe, maybe I might've heard others say that, I might."

"Well, then? Do you know him as Arcton?"

"I'm not outside a bargain, I'm not," he smiled politely to show his willingness to cooperate.

"Yes, well before we pursue *that* suggestion," McGurdy said, sensing he was onto something. "Have you ever seen anything like this?" He held out the cane.

"Mmmm. I might've maybe and maybe not've." and smiled again, a toothless smile.

"Tell you what," McGurdy said, "We can all but dismiss your charges *if* we get the information we're looking for. This is your chance, you're only chance."

"All the charges?" he asked.

"If you give us enough information—information we can use—then yes, all the charges."

"All right then, let's give it a go, we will."

"Any other names or aliases?" McGurdy asked the prisoner.

"Mmmm. A time or two, maybe. Nothing you'd know. Friends—" he glanced at me "—some friends, call me Skrimp."

Now I knew what was only a suspicion a few minutes before. This was the same person who led me to the place I'd slept in, at the abandoned warehouse.

"Now do you remember me?" I asked.

He rubbed his face again, as if trying to solve a problem. "Mmmm. We might've run into each other, maybe once or again," he looked down.

"And you were the one who so generously found a place for me to stay where, by the way, I almost lost my life."

"I was only doing my messenger service, I was."

"For whom?" McGurdy asked.

"For Mr. Billy," Skrimp said. "But I don' know anythin' about you being troubled during your stay, you know, you know."

"Troubled?" I asked. "You mean attacked."

"No, nuthin' about that."

"Did Mr. Billy—Arcton—that is, did he instruct you to lead Dorn to that deplorable section of town on the night in question?" McGurdy spoke up.

"Told me I'd be doin' 'em a favor, he did."

McGurdy, sensing he was on a hot streak, returned to the cane. "And what about this? Have you seen this before, or anything like it?"

"Boys have 'em."

"Boys? What boys? You mean like Cobb and Dilly?"

"Yeah, them. An' other ones too. They hang around the old ware-houses. Lots of curiosities there."

"What kind of curiosities?" McGurdy wanted to know.

"Strange goin's on. Unnatural. It's the noises at night mostly. I stay away from 'em, I do."

McGurdy took a deep breath. "Well, that's all for now. We'll conduct further investigations, and if you're telling the truth, you may be in better shape for it—better off then when you first stepped in here."

"Then you'll let me go?" Skrimp asked.

"Possibly. But I wouldn't be so quick minded about it. We may have other questions."

McGurdy escorted us to the main entrance.

"What is known about Arcton?" Reynold asked.

McGurdy looked puzzled. Then he motioned another officer over. He had been sitting behind the booking counter. McGurdy nodded once, looked the man in the eye, and that was sufficient encouragement to speak.

"He's the leader of The Brotherhood of The Perpetual Dawn," an organization we've not paid much attention to until recently. It's a spiritual society that preaches nativism," he said. "Arcton has managed to create a spiritual group with a mission. He's a nativist at heart," he said.

"A nativist." I repeated.

"Yes. A nativist is either a born American, or a sympathizer, threatened by new comers, immigrants who'll work for less wages, and who bring with them foreign beliefs and superstitions," the officer said. "It's the old story of the citizens born here who feel they have a rightful claim to what benefits them, and not outsiders. Makes for a bad mix. Combustible," he said sadly. "They've been skirmishes off and on. Rumors of rioting. Surely, you must have noticed."

"We took the back streets over here," Reynold said, "for that very reason."

"Smart of you," the officer said, "avoiding all that," then reached over to the registration counter, opened a drawer and pulled out a poster.

"If you want to know more about Arcton, you may want to attend this," and handed us the leaflet, an advertisement for an event. "They're all over town. You can't walk down Market Street without running into dozens of them. They're plastered all over."

McGurdy stared in awe at the poster.

"By the way," Reynold asked, "have you learned anything of Lippard's whereabouts?"

"Nothing new, I'm afraid. We've scoured the waterworks, the adjacent districts, even put the word out to our contacts. But nothing so far. Of course, we remain optimistic."

"Optimistic?" Reynold asked. "Why?"

"Because it's expected of us. How should the justice system function if it retires from its pursuits?" he asked. "The Public doesn't like to misplace its trust, and we like to keep it that way."

"Maybe you should follow up that question with your guest, Mr. Skrimp," Reynold suggested.

"That may be difficult. If he knows anything, he might not disclose it. He probably understands he would be considered an accomplice in his disappearance. Even failing to notify the authorities would have serious consequences, and even he must know that. But it can't hurt to follow up on your suggestion. We might get something out of him."

"Might I make another?" Reynold persisted.

"Another?" McGurdy asked dully.

"Why yes, another suggestion. Perhaps you could find a convincing volunteer to go under cover and infiltrate the ranks of Arcton's brotherhood."

There was a pause, during which time District Warden Chief McGurdy looked up to the ceiling, considering the proposition.

The booking counter officer stepped forward.

"If I may, Chief, I'd happily volunteer. Anything, you know, to put Arcton and his crew out of business."

"I appreciate your enthusiasm," McGurdy replied, and not wanting to appear eager to take up the idea said, "Let me give it some thought, but it does have some appeal." He considered the ceiling again.

"Of course," he paused in his contemplation, "you would need training in undercover stealth, and so on, but that shouldn't take long. As I said, let me give it some thought."

We left them at that point, McGurdy and his young officer—Sgt. James Tobin—I could see from his name tag—to ponder the possibilities of such an action as the one proposed by Reynold.

Soon as we went outside, we noticed the temperature had fallen sharply.

"Let's take the omnibus back, shall we?" Reynold asked. "I think we've had enough exposure for the morning. Ah!" he said, looking at his pocket watch, "It's nearing the hour. If we hurry we can catch the one that transfers up to Fairmount Avenue," he said of the horse-drawn carriages that carried as many as a dozen passengers at once.

Once we boarded, Reynold scanned the poster, then turned to me. "Here, you take this. Read it over. It could give us some helpful information, you know? Perhaps we could plan on attending," he said of the broadside. "Let me know what you think."

I nodded in agreement, and although I'd been listening to Reynold, I'd also been looking around the omnibus, or more precisely, at its passengers. They appeared drawn, nearly lifeless, much like—like— and here I said out loud: "The dreamless dead," and Reynold arched his brow and smiled at me.

"Exactly so my dear Dorn. Exactly so."

"And we—we are travelling with them?"

"It would seem that's the case. For the moment we are among them."

"Must we?" I asked. "Is there no alternative?"

Reynold chuckled. "No, no, we're getting off before they reach their final destination. Not to fear," and gave a reassuring smile.

*   *   *

BROTHERS OF PHILADELPHIA!

YOU ARE INVITED TO ATTEND

A MESSAGE ON
THE GREAT WORK

OR

THE REUNIFICATION

PRESENTED BY ARCTON, HEIR TO KELPIUS,
SACRED MONK OF THE WISSAHICKON

AT

THE CHESTNUT STREET THEATRE

ON

**SUNDAY, DECEMBER 3, 1843
AT 2:30 IN TH E AFTERNOON**

In the morning, the reading room has a rather soft light that assumes the various red hues of the drapes. I read Arcton's announcement, considered attending with Reynold, and when I was about to tuck it away, when I picked it up from the table, the light caught behind it somehow and it was then I realized it was not printed on cheap stock, common to public notices of the period pasted up on public buildings. This paper had some weight to it.

But that wasn't all. I held it up to the light and examined it further. I detected—ever so faintly—surely no one would find this unless they were carefully inspecting the paper—a miniature impression of those symbols we'd just been discussing that morning in McGurdy's station. There they were! In a chain that bordered the paper, and along with its barely detectable imprint, set back enough from the edge to escape notice by any ordinary reader.

I made a mental note to inform Reynold the next time we met, which, oddly, was within minutes of my finding the code, which I knew must somehow be related to the death of Eliza. There he was, standing by the sofa in the reading room, smiling.

"You've discovered something, Dorn?" he asked.

"Why yes, yes I have," I said, then showed him the announcement with its markings.

"What do you make of it?" Reynold wanted to know.

"Two things: this design indicates a strong and deep belief in the organization, and its sacred cause, and, the brotherhood must have considerable resources," I said.

"Exactly. And I agree. By resources you mean . . ."

"Capital," I replied.

"Enough to take on a fair share of operating the new *Stylus* I should think," Reynold said. "On another note, Poe is about make a second attempt to obtain the medication he lost in the storm, the treatment that could provide a cure for Virginia. Do you want to witness the event?"

"Do you have to ask?"

Without any more discussion on the matter, we were off, and the next thing I knew we were standing on a street corner in the publishing district.

"There," Reynold pointed across the street, "there is Poe coming out of the offices of Graham's Magazine. He has with him a check for the sale of a forthcoming short story. Not much by your standards, Dorn, but quite a bit for this period."

Poe paused. He looked down at the envelope in his hand, and was about to move on when something caught his attention. Standing on a median near an intersection, was none other than 'Frisco Red. He had scarves around his neck. Blue scarves, yellow scarves, gray scarves. He held some in his hands gracefully letting them float about his fingertips, calling out to pedestrians, how fashionable these were.

"Pure silk," he exclaimed, "fresh from the Orient. Ideal Christmas gifts. Celebrate the Holy Season with your loved ones in splendor! You cannot afford not to have one—or several for yourself or others!"

As Poe approached him, Reynold said, "There, you see he's trying to barter with the shaman for more medication. Of course, 'Frisco's reluctant: Poe must visit Sister Sarah at the Bottoms. Poe offers his payment he just received from Graham's, but 'Frisco shakes his head—no, it won't do. It must be something more substantial. Another poem then? No, even more than that. He has Poe in a corner now and he knows it and he wants to capitalize on Poe's neediness. Perhaps Poe could appeal for a loan. But he already owes most creditors in town, so much so, that he's considering filing for bankruptcy. There's an uncommon number of new books he's bought, some for review, but he pays for them nonetheless, a piano for Virginia, rent and other household expenses, and far too many costly visits from physicians."

We moved closer to the two men, enough to hear 'Frisco say, "There's no point in making the trip out to see Sister Sara, if you don't have anything for fair trade."

Poe didn't react. He couldn't say anything—he had nothing of value, except his writing and his faith in the future.

'Frisco sensed his vulnerability, and knowing the position he had put him in said, "Let's think our way out of this like two businessmen," and led him across the street so the two stood inside the doorway of a shop.

"Your name has value," 'Frisco said. "And that value could get you everything you want. What's the harm? Use your name. Use it to your advantage—and Virginia's."

Poe eyed him with suspicion. "If you have anything worth saying, say it then, and be clear," he admonished him.

"All right then. Lend yourself to what would do you the most good. Allow, if you will, those brave gentlemen who wish to give birth to *The Stylus* simply the use of your name, and Virginia will be forever grateful to you for doing so."

Poe stopped him with his hand; palm opened, within inches of his face, "No, that would disgrace us all, especially Virginia."

"Is dignity so dear?" 'Frisco asked, but he was speaking to the cold wind that blew down the street, for Poe had gone.

He stopped briefly at the bank, cashed his check, and was on his way to pay something on account with the coal distributor lest he fall behind his credit line, then stopped at a general store for lamp oil, and lastly he visited a dry goods establishment for yarn that Muddy had wanted for months.

*   *   *

The following days did not pass without a few notable events. Poe was immersed in drafting a long piece of fiction, rarely leaving his room. Then suddenly, one afternoon he complained to Maria of chills, and by evening had taken to bed. She regularly changed his warm compresses, but that was not her only task; Virginia had relapsed and was suffering a fever, so debilitating that Maria sent out for the physician who, after visiting with both Virginia and Poe, and after making his prescriptions, was on his way out, when he informed Maria he could not continue to offer treatment unless he received compensation long overdue, and suggested an associate, a herbalist who might be persuaded to visit the house if needed, at a reduced fee, but that was the best he could do, then waited a moment, turned, and said, "Herbal healing may be best. You will be in good hands. I'm sure of that," and managed a weak smile.

As he was leaving, George Rex Graham met him coming up the steps; tipped his hat, and greeted Muddy. He brought with him a box of pastries which he presented to her along with his wishes for Poe's recovery.

"My, this is so kind of you, Mr. Graham. I'm sure this will help get our dear Eddy up and about."

Again there was a tip of the hat; an understanding smile, and Graham was on his way, leaving Muddy to return to caring for her family; at this time, virtually two semi-invalids. Her days were full; often resorting to stealing herbs and vegetables from neighbors' gardens if they were away and could not be asked for a helping

hand, and doing laundry, which now included the boiling of bed-
sheets, twice daily wiping down chairs, table tops, hand railings,
and doorknobs with disinfectant, anything that would come into
human contact.

The afternoon was quickly approaching when I was expected to
attend Arcton's lecture with Reynold who said he would meet me in
the theatre lobby.

By now, I had heard so much of Arcton, I was eager to see him
in action. I left the little family—Virginia struggling to regain a re-
mission, which I learned, came as often as the following relapse was
sure to follow—her coughing, muffled and distant in the house, a
constant reminder of her mortality, wreaked havoc on Poe's nerves
for his devotion to her, and I soon found myself in the company of
several Philadelphian notables in the lobby of The Chestnut Street
Theatre, who, like me, had come to find out what the fuss was all
about.

I stepped away from Reynold who had struck up a conversation with a government official sent from the mayor's office, and
looked through the doors: the theatre was nearly filled to capacity,
and seated behind the podium, in a line across the stage were a cast
of Arcton's most loyal followers. They were dressed respectfully, each
in a three-quarters length dark jacket with cloth buttons, white high
wing collars and black velvet cravats tied in a bow. They appeared
to be upright citizens, dedicated to the mission of the brotherhood
and to the central figure of the gathering, who, at the moment was
behind stage rehearsing for the last time his presentation, or perhaps
his performance.

Certainly, every detail gave the impression of a formal occasion;
well organized, with the sedate air of propriety. This did not prevent
the stationing of police at critical places in the theatre. I suspected

that as many appeared in uniform—necessary to dampen overly enthused patrons—as there were others dressed as if they too were members of the general audience.

Reynold made arrangements for us to sit in the front row, and I noted several individuals in our section: there was Cobb and Dilly, again in respectable dress, Sergeant Tobin, who blended in, a new member of the tribe, Griswold along with some of his backers who came to see firsthand the man they had heard so much about, the man who offered significant financial support for *The Stylus* in exchange for a front page column in every issue extolling the virtues and goals of the brotherhood, and there, among them all, the unlikeliest of figures, 'Frisco Red, in a dark coat and top hat which he kept with him, resting it on his lap.

A dignified man, somewhat portly, rose from his chair on the stage, stepped over to the podium and began his introduction of the afternoon's featured speaker.

Arcton, he claimed, was the essence of the divine, taking the virtues of self-sacrifice, the mission of improving the public welfare, from his spiritual predecessor, that holy legend of the Pietist-monk of the Wisshakon, none other than Kelpius himself, who lived only to improve the spiritual and material lives of those in his religious community."

At this point, there was a burst of applause, and a few shouts of "Bravo, Bravo!!"

By the time the speaker left the podium, the crowd was sufficiently stirred, and welcomed Arcton with a standing ovation. Yet at the same time, I noticed men coming down both side aisles in single file, wearing white arm bands. Some carried placards.

Arcton raised his hands over the crowd, and when there was silence, began . . .

"Brothers, we are living in the time of trial and trepidation. While we try to purify ourselves so as to be worthy of our great fortune: to be reunified with our rightful place in the presence of celestial harmony, there are those about us who would take from us our material means, our self-sufficiency, our right to provide for ourselves and our families—"

Here, he broke off as there were sounds of disruption coming from those lines of men who had recently entered the theatre.

"Fraud!" one shouted out.

"You are an offense to God and man!" yelled another.

Arcton's men rose as if on signal and stood ready to expel the hecklers.

The protestors took this as a challenge and mounted the stage. Four of Arcton's men quickly surrounded their leader and led him off through one of the wings to an outside alleyway.

"Freedom for all under the law," one of the white-bands shouted, as someone pitched a fireball on stage. It rolled then burst into flame. The grand drapes were caught up in a wild blaze as theatregoers scattered, jamming the exits and the lobby doors.

The police attempted to restore order, but it was well beyond them. The fire brigade was called, and by the time it arrived, the theatre was emptied. There were a few brawls between Arcton's loyalists and the white-bands out on the street, but these were quickly subdued by McGurdy's men.

One of the officers dragged a man out of a skirmish by his coat collar and walked him over to McGurdy.

"Who are yuh then?" the officer asked, and when there only the look of anger and no answer, he shook him by the collar again and showed him his baton.

"I can crush your skull with this," he said, holding it within inches of his face, "and you'd regret it the rest of your life. Again, who are yuh then?"

The captured man caught his breath, still wild-eyed, and said, "We're all members of The Citizens's Workers League. We're rail workers, weavers, water pump operators, night watchmen."

"And just who heads up this . . . this . . . *league*," McGurdy asked.

"No one you'd know, or care to know," he said.

"Out with it," the officer threatened him again with his nightstick.

"A fairer man than any you've seen here today," he said. "And for all the good it'll do yuh, his name's Desmond O'Dell," then added, "we have the right to work, you know, and work without insults, or threats, or worse."

"Where do I find this O'Dell?" he asked.

"At the Naval yards," he replied.

McGurdy copied the name down in his pocket notebook, and with a motion of his hand, had the officer dismiss the protestor, who ran up the street to join a band who had been waiting for him, and then they all left the scene together, walking backwards, still yelling taunts and threats.

"Enough excitement for one afternoon," McGurdy said. "Best we all find our way to our homes," and was about to leave when one of his officers ran up to him.

"Chief, you have to come up to Fairmount Water Works immediately. There's been an . . . an incident."

"What kind of *incident*?" McGurdy asked.

"A most serious incident, sir," he replied. "You're needed at once."

*   *   *

THE SECOND DISCOVERY

When they stopped to tighten their laces, the young couple, laughing in the cold, looked over and there, in the shrubbery at the edge of an inlet on the river where they had been skating, was the body of a girl. They signaled others to join them, pointing to their find—another couple took a quick glance at the body—and left to summon the authorities immediately, while the young couple remained with the dead girl.

We went along with McGurdy and his patrol. It was nearing sunset, and the atmosphere was growing dim.

After observing the corpse, McGurdy turned to one of his men and said, "Get the coroner over here at once to examine this ... this wretched creature," then paused to take a deep breath.

There was the familiar red line across the throat which suggested a garroting similar to the first victim, but there was something even more disturbing. McGurdy pulled back some shrubs. The girl's face had been so disfigured it was beyond recognition. "This is a particularly gruesome display," McGurdy said.

"Yes," Reynold replied, "a display indeed. She's been positioned as in such a way to be found—not too obvious—but just enough to catch the attention of the skaters—then whatever was done to her face—as if it's been nearly dissolved—creates a macabre effect as if those responsible had not been satisfied with a capital offense, but gone to additional *lengths—completely unnecessary I might add—to create a grotesque effect. And there is this," he said pointing to the collar of her blouse.*

Reynold stepped into the bushes and when he attempted to remove the pin that attached the slip of paper to her collar, McGurdy intervened.

"That's quite enough," he said. "I'll see to that, and pushing Reynold off to one side, removed the note, read it, and said, "I suppose this means something, but it's so much gibberish to me. Here," he said sarcastically to Reynolds, "It's something that you might find relevant, I'm sure."

It was written in the same hand as the note left on Eliza White's body, another sestet penciled in rough lettering:

> *What is worse than one is two,*
> *& two will not face Dawn again,*
> *While her sisters mourn & wait,*
> *Wait & worry about their fate,*
> *How many more will there be*
> *Before Reason overcomes Obstinacy?*

McGurdy turned to his officers. "Stay with the body until the medical examiner arrives; accompany him to the city, and remain at the morgue until otherwise notified. We'll get to the bottom of this. I want to meet with coroner personally after he's had sufficient time to make his observations. The condition of the corpse is particularly troublesome."

McGurdy put his notebook back in his pocket, shivered once, and said, "Let's move on up to the pavilion for a brief chat, shall we? It should only take a minute," then looked at us both—Reynold and myself—as if to say, "This is not a suggestion."

We accompanied him up the hill, huffing all the way, the steam coming out of us like horses, and behind us, two lieutenants following the little group as if in the capacity of official escorts.

The pavilion, during this time of year, served as a warming house and was populated by Sunday skaters. We took a table near the window and could see the great expanse of the river below and some of the buildings of the water works, all fading into darkness.

McGurdy ordered hot cocoa; Reynold settled for a mid-grade tea—all that was available—the officers and I abstained.

Reynold insisted on calling the warming house, "The Belvedere," because of its views, obscured now by nightfall. Still, from our height we could look down on the skaters near the shore illuminated by gas lamps. Some skaters, the more daring of their lot, holding torches, moved farther out on the ice.

"It's important to place our suspects," McGurdy said. "This offense occurred just recently; I dare say during the time we were at Arcton's lecture—not his men, nor the white-bands could not have done this, not those present at the theatre anyway."

He pushed back his chair and went to one of the fireplaces near our table and warmed himself; first his hands, then he pulled up the tails of his long coat, bent over slightly and allowed the heat to attend the back of his thighs.

McGurdy glanced over at Reynold. "Where was your dear friend this afternoon?" he asked.

"My dear friend? " he seemed not to know what McGurdy was searching for.

"Yes, yes," he became impatient, "that fellow you dote over so much, you know, the poet."

"Poe?" Reynold said, and stopped himself from laughing. "You can't be serious. He would never do such a thing. He's much too weak at the moment, and besides it's entirely outside his nature. And what could possibly be his motive?"

"Sympathy?" McGurdy said. "Or something we haven't learned

yet. Oh," he said with exasperation, "who knows what's in the mind of a fellow like that."

"What do you mean?" Reynold baited him.

"What wild notions lurk in a head such as his? Why everyone knows how dark *his* thoughts are. What characters there are on paper are not far from the man who's created them," he added.

"I'm sure news of this atrocity will work its way back to Poe soon enough. I wish there were some way of keeping it from him. It will devastate him," Reynold said.

"Nonetheless," McGurdy went on, "I'm assigning men to the Spring Garden House. And you can tell Poe anything you like. Tell him it's for his own safety, and the safety of his family, but I want to know his whereabouts at all times from this point on, until we find exactly who is responsible for these hideous atrocities."

He reached inside his pocket and pulled out the note attached to the dead girl's body, then stripped a sheet from his pocket notebook and laid it on the table. "Here," he said to Reynolds, "you may copy this. Compare it to the verse found on Eliza White's person, and while you're at it, ask yourself how many murderers are inclined to write poems about their victims, then attach them to their bodies."

As we were finishing up—McGurdy draining his cocoa, and Reynold leaving most of his tea—a peace offering was made.

"In exchange for an interpretation of that note," he said, looking directly at Reynolds, "you and your friend here can attend my interview with the coroner, assuming you will keep such a meeting in the highest confidence."

We were all about to leave together as we had arrived at this place, this "Belvedere," when Reynolds pulled me aside: "Go back with the others. I—I wish to remain here for a while," he said.

And so I left him there, standing by the window, looking down from that height at the skaters below, gliding in the glow of those gas lamps positioned along the shoreline.

It has often occurred to me since, that Reynold's mercurial presence, his sometimes capricious behavior—I suppose that was the Mummer in him—for all of that, he was often morose, brought on by serving as an advocate for difficult, if not lost causes, as he was now, looking down into the darkness and the carefree skaters that seemed so far away.

*   *   *

When I returned to Spring Garden House, I had barely entered the reading room when Alana appeared. She stopped and looked in.

I had thrown my coat over a chair and was about to lie down on the sofa.

"I thought Reynold was with you," she said.

"He was, but he insisted on remaining at the Fairmount Park pavilion for a time."

"I see. Well, I can't stay," Alana said. "I'm late as it is. I have to get back home."

"Home?" I asked.

"Yes," she seemed amused, "I *do have* a job, you know."

"Ah, the job," I said trying to conceal my sarcasm. "It seems to me you might be spending more time here, attending to Sissy and Muddy than anywhere else."

"It may *seem* that way," Alana said, "but it's not that way. Not that way at all."

By now she had stepped inside the room.

"Look," I just want to know if Reynold is holding up after this last . . . this last . . ." she looked dejectedly down on the carpet.

"Of course," I said. "I understand."

She smiled. "I should be going—"

"You've must have been his associate for a very long time," I said, consciously knowing I was prying for more information and hoping at the same time Alana wouldn't suspect me of being too inquisitive of a personal relationship with Reynold.

"Yes, I've known Reynold for a very long time," she laughed a little. "Actually, I've known him for ages."

"And you're concerned about him?"

"Why of course. Aren't you?"

"In a way. I suspect he has resources to cope with his difficulties," and here I meant to say defense mechanisms, but prevented myself for some reason, perhaps I considered it a bit too personal.

"But not the kind you might imagine," she said. "He tires of human suffering, as we all do; the weight of its weariness. He once told me that 'if human suffering could be measured it would equal the weight of the world itself.'"

"Surely," I said. "But may I ask, how did you two come to know each other—how was it that you now work together?"

"Like you," she mused, "I was *recruited*, but I don't have time for details now," she waved her hand, "perhaps on another occasion we can have an in-depth discussion. Although I must say it seems as if things are going well with you two. He's very pleased with your progress and the way in which you might be of service to Poe. And as you might suspect, I am grateful as well," she smiled and with hand on the brass door lever was about to exit and close the door behind her, when I spoke up.

"You'll be returning soon?"

"As soon as I'm needed here," she said. Reynold will let me know. He's always been there for me when I've needed him, and I intend to return his loyalty whenever possible." She stopped a moment, looked away as if she was considering a thought, then looked directly at me.

"He will do the same for you someday."

"For me? How so?"

"What is your greatest desire?" she asked.

At the moment, I thought it might be to understand more about my own situation, and just as quickly put that thought out of mind, a bit amused with myself for having thought so, especially under the circumstances. "For the long term I suppose it would be achievements in my field."

"Example?"

"Well, come to think of it, just the other day Reynold and I were discussing the possibility of interactive holograms, or variants, something that we haven't been able to achieve yet—"

"You mean," she interrupted, "the interaction of the kind you have been experiencing here, the kind you've been seeing around you."

"Well, yes, I suppose, but there are so many refinements needed. Holograms require extended responses, textures; they need to carry electromagnetic DNA."

"Really?" Alana said. "Someday—and let's hope it's in the far distant future—having returned to your life and having made a success of this venture—explaining this dimension to others, redeeming Poe's character—you too will come to what all mortals come to, and there, when at last you begin to drift away, there at your side will be Reynold who will guide you so that any longing, or unfulfilled purpose may be once again pursued."

I had the sudden impulse to say something amusing, or so I thought. "Would that include you?" I asked.

She smiled, tilted her head a bit, and said, "We'll see," and quietly closed the door.

*   *   *

When Alana left, I wasn't alone for long. It seemed to be my evening for visitors. I heard some movement going on outside the reading room, and down the hall, there was Reynold fumbling with his Mummer's costume that he kept in a compartment off from the little visitor theatre where the film on Poe is shown. Apparently, he works on it during his down time, when the place isn't busy, and he can slip away from the other curators. He paints his headdress various colors, sews on sequins, and makes alterations as he goes along.

When he looked up, he was half in—and half out—of his street clothes.

"Dorn! You surprised me. I must get across town. Our division is having its last rehearsal before the holidays, then before you know it, it will be New Year's Day and the big parade! Ah," he stopped and looked upward, "Carn-i-val!"

"I'm glad you have an outlet, something that gives you a reprieve from your other responsibilities."

"Well, yes, Mummery is that. It has its roots in ancient lands. It's spread all over the world, you know. Momus is the Greek god of satire and mockery. This year, my division, The Fancies, allows for one Aztec fantasy witch doctor, and that's me!" He laughed. "It's all synchronized, so it's quite the spectacle. We have the royal dance of the scarecrows and a grand ball finale that has nuances of the best opera. You'll see," he said, certain that I would be attending. When he had changed, he paused. "I try to make them all," he said.

"All?"

"Yes, every year I try to make Notting Hill, the carnival at Venice, the Mardi Gras, Rio, and I have my favorites, of course."

"Of course."

"By the way," he added, "on a more serious note, I understand that McGurdy's men have rounded up the captain of The Citizen's Workers League and have placed him in a holding cell down at the district ward, on the charge of suspicion of collaborating in a public assault and the willful destruction of property. He's to be interrogated in the morning. Let's plan on going, shall we?"

*　　*　　*

McGurdy was seated at a table with an officer on either side of him; one for protection—a protocol measure—should the prisoner become suddenly aggressive, which wasn't likely since he was in shackles, and another officer—a district staff sergeant—to take notes.

Reynold and I occupied a far corner.

McGurdy's chair squeaked as he adjusted himself. "For the record then, you are . . ."

"Desmond O'Dell," the prisoner replied.

"And you are employed?"

"I work at the Naval yard."

"How long have you worked there?" McGurdy asked.

"Two years now," was the reply.

"Federal job. You're one of the lucky ones. The bureaucrats running that place rarely give employment opportunities to foreigners," he said.

"I'm second generation," O'Dell clarified.

"Even second generation," McGurdy replied. "What kind of work do you do at the Naval yard?" he asked.

"I'm a joiner by trade, but they won't use me for that. Instead, I'm given freight hauling work to do much of the time, loading and unloading building materials on the docks."

McGurdy looked at him. "Hard work. Looks like you're built for it. Now," he said while he picked up a file from his desk, "I understand you're a family man."

O'Dell nodded his head.

"Ohh," McGurdy feigned pity, "and with wee ones too, I suppose."

"Yes, two."

"So why should a family man take on risky business—and I'm not talkin' about your employment," McGurdy said.

"Because we cannot continue to live with tyranny."

"We?"

"We. We are all brothers."

"Ohh, are we now?" McGurdy baited him.

"Yes, and you should know the hardships we've had to face."

McGurdy squinted his eyes. "*We* may have our mother country in common, but know you are on one side of the law, and I'm on the other, surely as there's this desk between us."

He shuffled through some papers in the file. "This league of yours, what is it then? Some kind of union?" McGurdy asked.

"You might say as much."

"*I* might say? It's not for me to say, Mr. O'Dell. Don't play coy. We have some of your brawlers locked up down the hall, and if you want them back in your ranks, you'll cooperate.

Is that understood?"

"It is," he said with reluctance.

"These charges are serious," McGurdy said, "there's restitution to be made; fines to pay. One of the most fashionable buildings in Philadelphia, the pride of our cultural community, must be restored, and why? Because of your tribe of hooligans, that's why," he shook his finger at him, then paused, took a breath and asked, "Explain this league of yours."

"As you suggested, it's a union, a union of men who only wish to live and work in the absence of oppression of every kind. Many of us cannot find decent employment, and when we do, torment is our lot—from employers, co-workers—we are confronted by hatred for us—and our cause: equal rights protected by law."

"I understand," McGurdy said. "And you're willing to risk your very livelihood; your family's health and safety for this cause of yours?"

"I am," he replied.

McGurdy considered this for a moment. "Then you're a fool," he said.

Reynold turned to me, "Perhaps he is a fool in the way an ethical man is a fool, and if he is a fool he is a noble fool," he whispered.

McGurdy was about to return to the crime in question when his chair squeaked again. This time, the officer assigned to guard the prisoner stepped out into the hall and came back with a replacement. "This one's a bit sturdier, sir," he said.

McGurdy accepted the exchange, then asked, "Were any of your followers up at the Fairmount Park Water Works last Sunday afternoon?"

"I couldn't say. Our league does not inquire into what our members do in their own time."

Here, the staff sergeant who had been taking notes, moved over, cupped his hand and whispered in McGurdy's ear.

"And you, Mr. O'Dell," McGurdy said, clearing his throat, "were you at The Chestnut Street Theatre, or perhaps in the vicinity of Fairmount Park that afternoon?"

"No, sir." he replied.

"Hmmm," McGurdy mused, "Of course not. Home with family, I suppose."

"Yes, exactly so."

"Is it now? While your followers were disrupting a public gathering, threatening peaceful citizens, and firebombing The Chestnut Street Theatre, you were keeping the company of friends and family who would so attest."

"That is correct," O'Dell said.

"Do you know why we are concerned of your whereabouts?"

"I have heard, and cannot confirm, but based on rumor, there was a most heinous act committed at the place you mentioned. But why would you think that I, or for that matter, the league's members would be involved in something so abhorrent?"

McGurdy paused and looked over to his sergeant, who again, whispered in his ear.

"Those whom you claim are tormenting you and your league are those who are inspired to do so by the likes of Arcton and his crowd, and you must know as well, that it is he who is under suspicion for willful homicide—and you, or one of your men, may have taken the opportunity to commit second crime to heighten our investigation into Arcton's Brotherhood—to throw off us off *your* track," McGurdy said, "and thus weaken his organization, disgracing him and his pursuits for the benefit of you and your league."

"I cannot imagine any of those I know, those dedicated to our cause, would murder a young woman just beginning her life," O'Dell replied.

"Let's hope for your sake, you are correct," McGurdy warned. Then he pushed back his chair and turned to his note taker and said, "Enough for today. Put Mr. O'Dell back in confinement, but keep him separate from his brawlers. And no visitors."

He rose, and stepped over to O'Dell. "We're not done with you, and if there is anything you may have forgotten to tell us, maybe it will come to mind when you have sufficient time by yourself to think it through."

McGurdy was about to leave the room when the prisoner spoke up, "May I ask, have you found Lippard?"

"Lippard? Why do you ask? What is Lippard to you?"

"His reputation is great among my followers. As a labor league reformer, he is hero to us all."

"That may be, but for the men of my ward, we're engaged in a manhunt that should show results presently."

"As are we," O'Dell replied.

McGurdy, flushed with aggravation, shot back: "You and your kind stay out of police matters. The whereabouts of George Lippard is our affair and ours alone."

*   *   *

The coroner's office was located just inside the city line, in a low-rent section. On the way over, Reynold said, "We've been working on this fellow."

"Working?" I asked.

"Yes, some of the others in my division and I, we've been trying to recruit him."

"Recruit him for what?" I asked.

"For Mummery no less. He *needs* to be a Mummer. His job requires it. Can you imagine how glum and discouraging it must be to work with corpses all day? I can't. We thought—the boys and I—" he said referring to his brigade members, "that Dr. Warren would make a fine harlequin. Oh, it might take some time, but we have that, and I'm optimistic of the outcome of our efforts."

Bizzare as it seemed, Reynold was correct; from the moment we entered the office of Dr. Warren, I could tell he was in need of a lifestyle change. He was suffering from congestion, a head cold was my guess, and kept dabbing his nose with some bunched up gauze which was probably easily available as he might have use for it in his practice. His face was red and puffy, especially his nose, which I attributed to his head cold, and otherwise his appearance was, more or less, what one might expect; a bit overweight from lack of activity, I suspect; his hair disheveled, and his white medical coat had seen better days, otherwise he seemed to have the patience and practicality his profession required.

No sooner had we entered his office, and he was about to take a seat behind his desk, he left had to answer the brass bell on his door. It was McGurdy accompanied by two officers.

"Ah," he said, taking off his long coat, "I hope you haven't begun without us."

"No, no, not at all," Dr. Warren assured him, "we were just getting started."

At that moment, the office door swung open and there appeared a younger man, an apprentice would be my guess, who said, "Doctor, the bodies are ready for viewing. I've removed them from storage to our examination room."

Dr. Warren nodded in acknowledgement, then began, "Our postmortem examinations require notes on the condition of the deceased, cause of death, and other pertinent information.

We've determined the victim's height, weight, race, approximate age, and we have made every attempt to identify her person, and have failed. Well, let me show you—" he said, and led the group down a corridor into the display area. There were two bodies, each on a stainless steel medical table, side by side.

Dr. Warren made some motion with his hand, and at the same time called for "Fenn." This brought his apprentice over with a wooden pointer with a rubber tip. Warren used this to lift the sheet of the most recent victim.

"The face is so disfigured it is impossible for us to identify the subject. This act would not have been enough to cause death, and we must conclude was done after the fact, and for an unknown reason. Our best guess is that this was done with photographic acid, or some equivalent. And here," he used the pointer again, "you see again the use of a garrote."

"It seems it was done all the more to torment Poe," Reynold spoke up. "The brutishness of the crime—it's excess—alone would be enough to debilitate anyone who knew the woman. In addition, not being able to identify the victim, especially in Poe's case, worsens the agony."

We waited for someone to respond. McGurdy jotted something down in his notebook. The intern cocked his head and looked at Dr. Warren as if to say, "What now?" And after a period of silence, the coroner began again: "Unlike Eliza here—the other victim—" he pointed to the second sheeted body, "this one was subjected to greater trauma, however, there are bits of tree bark and plant debris, as you can see," he pointed to her hair, "and what I suspect are twig scratches on her face and arms, suggesting the body was dragged to the area in which she was found. Therefore, it is unlikely the murder was committed by the shore at Fairmount Park, but somewhere else. My guess is that she was positioned in such a way as to be discovered, but of course, that is the province of the authorities," he said with a nod to McGurdy, "and something not to be decided here."

"I agree," McGurdy spoke up. "What is more important," he said, "is the identity of this regrettable creature. At the moment, that is our priority. There must be something that would reveal her to us."

"I may be able to help," Reynold said, "but it might take a few days."

"Let's hope you find a lead," McGurdy said. "You've had time enough with the note found on the victim which sounds strangely familiar, as if perhaps your poet wrote it?"

"Poe? Never. It doesn't scan like his verse, for one thing—"

"Nonetheless, he's still a suspect," McGurdy reminded us. "So tell us, what's the message pinned to this poor girl's body that's so important?"

Reynold removed his copy of the note from his jacket pocket. "Loosely put, it tells us this death was avoidable; that it was obstinacy that was its cause, and that others may follow. It is something Poe would understand best, since it seems to be directed to him. If he does not come to his senses and agree to Griswold's terms for *The Stylus*, other deaths are inevitable."

"You have me thinking Poe could very well be writing to himself were he the perpetrator. Ah," McGurdy's finger went in the air as if he had discovered something, "but that's *exactly* what a clever madman would do to throw us off his track, now isn't it?" He smiled with confidence, summoned his aides, and left the building.

When Fenn, the dutiful intern, who seemed to be keenly attentive to every aspect of our meeting, accompanied us down the corridor, and after he had closed the door behind us, I asked Reynold how he planned to learn of the dead girl's identity.

"I want to ask Alana; see if she would be willing to convince Virginia to reconvene the assembly of women, the same circle that gathered after the death of Eliza. Then we could see who is there and who is not. Up until now there has been one empty chair, once occupied by Eliza White, and at the next assembly there will be two. The identity of the second victim will be determined by who—among the women—is missing."

*   *   *

Once the backers of *The Stylus* understood Arcton's agenda—a utopic spiritual community disguising its real purpose of hate and nativism—they convened an assembly of their own in the loft of the Eulogy tavern.

I was at a table reading the evening newspaper when Marcel came over in his waiter's waist apron, his pencil and pad at the ready.

"Good to see you, Dr. Dorn," he said. "You've been well I take it?"

"Yes, thank you."

"It's been some time since you've visited us. What would you like this evening?"

"Information."

The pencil and pad went back into the pocket of the apron and Marcel crossed his arms. "What kind of information?"

"I'd like to know more about Griswold and his investors, in light of recent events."

"By recent events, do you mean Arcton's reception at The Chestnut Street Theatre? That seems to be the talk of the town."

"Yes, of course, and how it might affect their plans for *The Stylus*."

"That shouldn't be too hard to provide," Marcel smiled, "if you come with me, I'll show you what you want to know," and with that I followed him up the narrow staircase to Eulogy's loft, where I first saw the investors who wished to finance *The Stylus*.

Soon as I saw the group, I turned to thank Marcel, but he had gone.

Graham spoke for the rest of them who sat silent. "We'll not let our names become soiled by an anarchist," he said directly to Griswold.

Griswold protested: "It's not what you think. Arcton's popularity is rising throughout the city, and soon, the state, and then the country! You don't understand his influence—the power of his expression. His power to persuade, it is—it is—limitless!"

"That may be so, but we have our own reputations to consider," Graham said, with the other investors nodding in agreement. "As for Arcton, you, my dear Griswold, you seem to be under his spell."

"I assure you that is not the case. I regard this as a business venture only, one in which Arcton is willing to assume both risk and capital. I don't know how we can refuse his contributions."

"Is it true," Graham went on, "that he—or his band—may be responsible for the recent murders of the two young women we've been hearing so much about? That these heinous acts were committed solely for the purpose of persuading Poe to consent to his role as co-publisher?"

"Conjecture," Griswold shot back. "It's only the clumsy ill-informed speculation of those who are at a loss for any other explanation, and they chose the easiest target. There is nothing to indicate Arcton was behind these vicious acts. None at all."

"Have you read one of these columns he's proposing?" Graham asked.

"A copy should be in my possession shortly. I understand he has been preparing a draft for the first issue."

"I suggest you secure a copy before we go any further, and submit it to those present here."

"I—I'll try . . ." Griswold replied.

"I'm afraid you must do more than *try*, my friend. The future of our collective contributions to *The Stylus* depend on it," Graham said, then he considered a moment, "The holidays are approaching. You have until the end of the month—let's make it the first of the New Year then—and if we don't have Arcton's inaugural message to our subscribers, then we will be forced to reconsider our investment. Is that understood?"

There was a moment's pause, then the investors rose almost as if at once, and the entire group, including Griswold, vanished, and I stood alone in an empty room.

*   *   *

The Christmas season was upon us—what the townspeople call "The Holy Days"—when the commerce of the city slows, and people, when they went out at all, to market or services, scurried back quickly to the peace of hearth and home.

Everything seemed to lack movement, as if daily pace was subtracted from human affairs. The snow fell quietly, in slow motion, even the rivers themselves that flanked the old city moved sluggishly with ice. As for me, I spent most of the Christmas season indoors, rarely leaving the Spring Garden reading room, and seldom did I venture outside, and then just long enough to note the calmness of the atmosphere, the sense of solace itself.

McGurdy's guards remained posted outside each door, and were relieved every eight hours around the clock. During their shifts, Muddy regularly took out cups of tea, but her offerings were politely declined as if the guards were of a mind fixed on duty alone, impervious to the cold and damp. Their brother officers were out scouring the city for Lippard—and for his abductors. The same could be said for O'Dell's men, for they too had an interest in finding their hero of workers' rights.

The Poe house was quiet for the most part, allowing for Muddy's humming in the kitchen, Virginia's occasional cough, or Catarina prowling about, meowing for attention or scraps. Edgar kept to his writing room, rarely coming downstairs.

Christmas eve found the family gathered around the fireplace. The presents were simple, "homespun" as Muddy put it. She had knitted a gray scarf for Poe; Sissy had given her mother a sampler, and in return, she received a comb. Poe gave his wife a small vile of lavender perfume, and Catarina was given a cat bell so she wouldn't be wandering off. Poe received a plated nib for his dip pen, "the latest on the market," as Maria and Virginia were quick to note, and then everyone gathered around the piano that Poe had rented to sing Christmas carols.

Later, there were cups of cocoa with shredded bits of chocolate. Sissy had a new piano score loaned from a neighbor, and she was about to play it when Poe complained of a malady, it was "the ague again, that persistent imp of aggravation," that so disrupted his attention he had to excuse himself and left his little family to retire upstairs. There, he could not calm his chills and called out for another blanket.

It was during this period that I was struck with a unique clarity of mind; I realized I was committed to pursuing Poe's cause as much as Reynold or Alana with whom I shared that distinct mutual passion that binds humans who share a common mission, but also a rare sense of camaraderie.

I never considered myself a supporter of causes. I am a man of science—there I said it—I am not a literary man, and I do not have any special feelings for those who pursue literary ambitions. I can't say I am more likely to help one person over another; the stranger on the street selected at random, was until now, as likely to receive my attention as my dearest friend. Given this—my central nature—it then seemed odd to me, no, more than odd, paradoxical, that I had become so involved in this most passionate of pursuits, to somehow correct those most atrocious wrongs done to Poe during his lifetime, and just as perplexing was my affinity for Reynold and Alana—my compassion for their loyalty to our mutual cause, and for those treasured women who had devoted themselves to Poe in life, and now, in death. I concluded that I must accept the enigma of knowing there were forces behind my will—a will I once believed was mine and mine alone—directing me on this most challenging, and dangerous course.

My nature then, had itself been changed, and those changes seemed as natural to me as if they were my own. This was a mystery to me and I judged it would remain so, until such time—would there ever be such a time?—when I could gather enough information to unravel it, and see it clearly for what it was. But that was the scientist speaking, and not the person I found in myself in the little reading room in the Spring Garden House during the Holy Days in Philadelphia in the winter of 1843.

*   *   *

I awoke much too early one morning, and as I was drifting back to sleep, heard a tapping on the window of the reading room. I rolled over and tried to ignore it, thinking it might be a branch in the wind, or the pecking of a bird. When it persisted, I threw back the quilt, went to the window, drew back the drapes and there staring at me was the face of Reynold, still clicking the glass with his knuckle.

When I lifted the pane he said, "Our informant—Jimmy Tobin—the one who's worked himself into Arcton's confidence and is becoming a member of that brotherhood, is about to report to an undercover officer from the ward who's assigned to the investigation. I was tipped off by a friendly connection I have in McGurdy's office—Perkins—you remember, he helped fend off your attackers when you were in the warehouse district. I thought you might want to see this first hand."

I hurriedly dressed and met Reynold outside. Before I knew it, we were moving down a deserted alleyway until we came to two men in the recess of a delivery bay behind a boarded-up shop.

As we approached, we heard them discussing Arcton's Brotherhood.

". . . and there I was," Sgt. Tobin was saying, "right in the middle of the lot of them, a column on either side all armed with those special canes, chanting their slogans about their divine rights, and filial loyalties as they initiated me with those damned canes. Oh, I have welts on the back of me to prove it. In six months' time I will no longer be a novitiate, and then in a formal ceremony, I too will receive a cane as well, and just as decorative as any we've seen," he looked nervously around, eager to divulge what he had learned then return to another job the ward found for him—as an apprentice weaver—all the time using his false identity.

The other officer quickly jotted down the information, trying to keep up with Tobin's rate of speech.

"The formal induction includes a tattoo as well," Tobin confided.

"Tattoo, you say?" the liaison asked.

"Yes," once a novice takes his oath to the Brotherhood, he is branded so to speak. All members have them—a circle of those same symbols found on their canes—the declaration of perpetual dawn through suffering for their divine mission—placed around the muscle of the upper right arm. It's quite the ritual, and when your time comes, it's done by the cane maker."

"The cane maker," the officer repeated.

"That's right. He's a big surly fella'—a sea faring man. And make sure," Tobin continued, "you note those canes aren't just used for initiations, they're used to purify the soul by purifying the body. It's a principle of the brotherhood.

Arcton will do anything to expand his order and its membership that's based on a doctrine of hate. Their goal is to become a political force and to do that they plan to take over the unions—to control the weavers, the naval yards, the coal transports, and any occupation where laborers feel threatened by outsiders.

Those they suspect of disloyalty, or those who are considered accursed, are subject to caning in an elaborate ceremony from which they never recover. When there is such an occasion, the members deliver equal blows so as to be mutually responsible. They wear hoods to hide themselves and to share the deed equally. Less regret, I suppose, if they feel any regret at all. In this way they conceal their identity from any possible retribution. Arcton has them thinking their doings are divinely inspired. I've heard—rumor mind you—that was the fate of the Poe women."

"Were you able to determine the identity of the second victim?"

"Not as yet, but soon I expect someone will say something. You can't associate with that group without picking up all kinds of talk. And by the way, Arcton's Brotherhood isn't just for backwaters and dullards. I've heard—but not yet seen—pillars of the community in their fold—respectable businessmen, civic leaders including councilmen, and union organizers, even some of the more prosperous attorneys.

Tobin looked around again. "All right. You have your information. Make sure it gets to McGurdy," and turned to go.

The other officer reached out and grabbed his sleeve. "Wait," he said, "we still don't know where these meetings are held."

"In the old warehouse district," Tobin said.

"Impossible. We've searched that area, and turned up nothing. There are only run-down buildings, vacant for the most part."

"Ah," Tobin said with some amusement, "so you would think. But go down a block directly southeast of the old warehouse district and you'll find a ruin of a house. Down cellar a stairway opens into a tunnel that goes directly underground to the site well below the floors of the buildings themselves. That tunnel is big enough to allow four horses side-by-each to pass thorough it easily, then it opens into a cavern with two levels; one for services and oratory; the other for scourging. On the lower level there's a concrete square with a stone kneeler, and chains anchored on either side with iron wrist locks. It's a sinister site, especially if you consider what's been done there."

"The women?" the officer asked.

"I fathom as much. And others too that we have yet to learn of—outcasts of the brotherhood for one slight or another. If they continue to acquire strength unchecked, I no doubt suspect Mr. O'Dell himself might find himself at the devil's altar."

"Any word of Lippard?" was the officer's last question.

Tobin shook his head and appeared grim; with that, the officer released his grip on his sleeve, and Tobin was off down the alleyway.

We were watching him as he receded in the distance, when Reynold said, "Maybe we are looking in the wrong direction."

"What do you mean?" I asked.

He nodded and looked in the opposite direction, and there far down the alleyway, peering from the sides of a pile of crates were two figures; only their stocking caps visible.

"Who might *they* be?" Reynold asked, as if to himself.

"I have no idea. We should try to catch up with them."

"Ah, we would be quite a pair; the two of us trying to subdue a couple of muscular young thugs," Reynold mused. "My guess is those men are no less than those who once accosted you, my friend."

"You mean Cobb and Dilly?" I asked.

"Precisely. They know these environs better than anyone, and they're no strangers to providing surveillance for the brotherhood. In any case, we can assume our dear Sgt. Jimmy Tobin has been followed, and that he has been followed all along. This was his first meeting, and now that they're onto him, who knows what will happen? I'll report the incident to McGurdy immediately," he paused, and glanced again down the alley. "There's something amiss—I sense it—something out of place. Once having tracked Tobin here, why would they have stayed? Unless they mean to do him harm. But for all they know, Tobin could have been meeting with anyone about anything. And they are not so hidden as to be beyond detection."

*   *   *

"The Investigator," District Warden McGurdy, his feet propped up on his desk, his half-eaten lunch on a tray along with the daily newspaper, was manipulating a tooth pick trying to dislodge a piece of beef packed between two molars, when Reynold and I entered his office.

He stopped at once, took his feet off his desk, flicked the tooth pick into a waste basket, cleared his throat and said, "He beat you to it."

"Who?" Reynold asked, "beat us to what?"

"Our liaison, of course. He just left my office, and once he's back in uniform will return to regular duty. I'm surprised you didn't bump into him as you came in. We know about our dear sergeant's peril."

"How so?" Reynold asked.

"Our liaison spotted the two ruffians who were trailing Tobin. It was too late for him to do anything but carry on the meeting as if it were simply two old chums running into one another—although in a questionable locale, I dare say. In any case, I've already sent a messenger to our informant, so that he might discontinue his association with the brotherhood and return here at once for a briefing and another assignment, one not nearly as dangerous."

"Now," he said, moving half-eaten beef sandwich toward him, "I have other business, however, if you gentlemen care to remain to learn first-hand of our runner's report, you may wait out by the registration desk. He should be back presently with our dear Sergeant Tobin, to the safety and security of this station."

We went out to the booking area and Reynold made small talk with the officer on duty; I looked at wanted posters, and took a little tour around the station. I found myself quite by accident in large room, a storage facility open to the hallway. There, among a row of lockers, I saw one of McGurdy's officers tucking away his wool street coat, then removing a police officer's tunic with its brass buttons from his locker. He was wearing a thin, white short-sleeved undershirt, and there, about his bicep tattooed in black ink were those same symbols found on the canes issued to Arcton's men at their induction, and as I had seen myself on the poster announcing his lecture at The Chestnut Street Theatre.

Imagine my surprise to learn of this, but then when that officer turned so I could see his three-quarter profile, to my horror I recognized him at once. It was the liaison officer who had met with Sgt. James Tobin less than an hour earlier.

I summoned Reynold immediately and by the time it took him to come to my side, the officer buttoned his tunic, secured his cloth-covered helmet, and left the room letting himself out through a back door.

We removed ourselves to the registration area and before we could discuss the matter, a young man rushed through the door out of breath and straight to the booking desk where he asked to see Warden McGurdy.

McGurdy turned sideways in his chair, able to see the front desk through the half-way opened door—as we could see him—peering at us. "Ah, our runner has returned already. In here, in here," he called out, snapping his fingers.

"Sir," the boy said, "I could not find Sergeant Tobin anywhere— not in the apartment that the ward secured for him, not at his place of work, not even down by the old warehouse district."

"Perhaps you need to look again," McGurdy said tersely. He couldn't have vanished, you know. Wait until nightfall, then have another go at it. He's probably out at the market, or with his family; I understand he has an aging father who has taken ill and he may be paying him a visit. Tobin will show up, and when he does, you're to see to it that he reports to the station at once. You, my dear lad, are expected to escort him here—hand in hand if you must."

When the boy left the office, Reynold leaned over McGurdy's desk and bent forward. "You have been intent on infiltrating Arcton's Brotherhood, but have you ever considered his brotherhood infiltrating *you*?"

*   *   *

Once out on the street, Reynold began to laugh. He could hardly contain himself; he was half doubled over in mirth.

When he came around again, I asked him the cause of his amusement.

"That—that—so-called 'investigator' in there," he said pointing back to the station is under the impression that Arcton's followers—namely Cobb and Dilly—are Tobin's undoers, when in fact, it is one of his own men, a member of Arcton's tribe no less, and actually selected by McGurdy himself as his trusted liaison! I can only wonder," he said, catching his breath, "how many more are in his ranks. And he hasn't the slightest idea," he laughed again. "Cobb and Dilly were plants. The liaison officer knew they were in the area, and detracted McGurdy's attention by 'informing' on them. They could also provide protection for their fellow brother—the liaison officer—should Tobin have become suspicious of him, and perhaps thinking he had exposed his cover, and once the liaison officer reported to the brotherhood, there would be severe consequences, Tobin might try to subdue him, and in that event even the slightest gesture from the liaison officer—a movement of his hand—would have brought the two thugs running to his aid. Now Arcton knows for certain that Tobin is a spy revealed by an officer who McGurdy thinks is one of his finest!"

"Shouldn't we tell him—tell McGurdy?" I asked.

"What? So he could make another blunder? Besides, who knows to what degree his ward is infested? McGurdy's unpredictable, and for all anyone knows, he could call together the entire force and find those who are in sympathy with Arcton outnumber those opposed. No, I'll not take a chance on that. What's done is done. They've outed Tobin, and they'll do the same to anyone else who's infiltrated their ranks, which makes me wonder about O'Dell's men, and how they're faring in *their* undercover attempts."

*   *   *

Virginia Clemm Poe, having reconvened the assembly of women

as suggested to her by Alana, encouraged to do so by Reynold for the purpose of learning the identity of the second victim, removed a folded paper from the inside of the full of her sleeve, and read:

My Dearest Sisters,

To those whom I love beyond life itself, to those who have committed themselves to the most honorable of causes, the purity of the purpose of language's highest intent, and who have been true to me in death as in life, please cease your efforts in following my pursuits in the face of overwhelming adversity, and agree to disband, for I cannot continue our association, not with any one of you, for you are at lethal risk as a result of my convictions. May you depart with my blessings, knowing you have served Honor.

Forever Yours,
Edgar

The room was quiet only for a moment, then the murmuring began as each woman turned to the other. Eventually, one stood and went from woman to woman, bending over and speaking in whispers, until she conferred with every member in the group, then addressed Virginia and Alana.

"I speak for this assembly, and for our departed sisters," here she glanced over to the two empty chairs, "and with their consent of all present. We are of a mind: to abandon our mission would be a disgrace we could not endure, and it would leave us without purpose in this world we now share and to which we have come to vindicate Principle and to restore Honor."

She moved forward, cupped her hand and whispered in Virginia's ear, then when she turned to the group, they all rose at once, and left the room.

We were waiting downstairs in the reading room for Alana.

When she entered, she announced: "They have all decided to remain in support of Edgar," she said somewhat beside herself, closing the door behind her.

"I want to believe," she continued, "their decision was based solely on their dedication to correcting those injustices inflicted upon the one whom they love, their Eddy, and to prevent *The Stylus* from poisoning the souls of the community—perhaps the nation—or if Arcton had his way—the world. And I believe that is true. It is also true that failing to complete the purpose that brought them here would mean oblivion. Where would they go, and what possibly could they pursue? What they have chosen to do, they must do.

The ladies consented to having as their spokesperson none other than Sarah Whitman, the senior member of their party and a devotee of Poe, his last great love to whom he was engaged before he died."

"And now do we know who should have occupied the second chair?" Reynold asked.

"We do. All the women confirmed it. The body which lies next to Eliza's at the coroner's vault is none other than a boyhood love of Edgar's, perhaps his first, the young mother of his schoolmate, the woman for whom he wrote the poem "To Helen," Jane Stanard. She died young, just over 30, and like the others, when called out to support Poe, she answered only to suffer this last, final death. For Poe, who was only 14 when he met her, she was to him a confidante, fantasy love, surrogate mother, and an aesthetic ideal."

"The medical examiner needs to be contacted soon as someone can be sent over," Reynold said.

"Yes," Alana agreed, "and the ward should be notified as well."

"Our friend McGurdy," Reynold said reluctantly, "yes, I suppose he must know," he looked up weakly, "Is there no end to this?"

Alana came over to the couch and sat next to Reynold. She placed her hand on his knee.

"I have a plan," she said, "but I want your blessing should I—we—decide to carry it beyond this reading room."

"Please," Reynold said, "anything, if it can possibly help put an end to these horrors and save Poe from the ultimate failure of—of everything."

Alana had been speaking to one of the women for some time, off and on, "Fanny Osgood," she said, "more than a mutual acquaintance of Griswold and Poe. Griswold was jealous of her relationship with Edgar. I should add that she may have been the only woman Poe was ever intimate with, if we exclude his wife, of course. That fact alone drove Griswold to portray Poe unfavorably whenever he had the chance, and then he would attack his character, often maliciously and without sufficient grounds.

What Fanny has proposed was this: if it would stop Griswold from extorting Poe—trying to force him to assume the role of co-publisher of *The Stylus* thereby endorsing Arcton's racial nativist agenda, his hate mongering by interacting with Arcton's Brotherhood to commit these heinous crimes against Eliza White and Jane Stanton—then she would attempt to convince Griswold of her affections toward him over anyone else in her life. Once that was accomplished, and he had been persuaded that her attentions were genuine and sustaining, she would convince him to cease his persecution of Poe and to abandon his determined attempt to profit from Arcton's funding of the project, and to rely on what capital was available; install Poe as co-publisher, quit all other demands, and move on from there.

Alana waited a moment for Reynold to consider this.

"She could be putting herself in danger," he said

"I don't understand," Alana said.

"Griswold is the most vindictive of men; history has proven that, and if by chance he should learn of Fanny Osgood's attempt to manipulate him, he could easily have her eliminated by Arcton's men. Fanny Osgood could very well be the third victim."

*   *   *

As it turned out, the third victim was not yet another homicide, but in an odd twist, Poe himself. It happened this way: Rex Graham, Poe's former employer, did care for the poet despite their many differences, even when he replaced Poe as an editor of his magazine with none other than Rufus Griswold; Graham would often go out of his way for Poe and his little family.

It was on one such occasion that Graham, learning he been given theatre tickets to a popular play, a comic farce, "Glance at New York," thought he would pass them on to Poe so he could lighten his domestic life for a few hours, and remove his mind from the grim realities he had been facing by taking Virginia and Maria to the theatre for the evening.

The trio left their house on the night of the opening, walked a few blocks to where the omnibus stopped on its way on the theatre, boarded, and were on their way downtown to the attend the play.

Later that evening when they returned, the house being empty several hours, Maria and Virginia went to the kitchen to fill the kettle for tea and set out a few pieces of fruit bread and the remainder of some jam left in a glass jar, while Edgar, waving off the refreshments, walked upstairs to his study, saying he was behind the deadline on a review, and it needed his attention.

The door was closed, not unusual, but Catarina the tortoise-shell tabby lay curled in a ball, purring. She blocked the poet's path to his room. When he approached her and gestured for her to move, she stopped purring and stared directly at him, into his own eyes.

Poe bent over to pick her up and she pressed herself closer to the door, and when he finally took her in his hands she squirmed and yowled as if her removal was something she vehemently protested.

Still clutching the cat to his chest, he used his right hand to open the latch to his study, then pushed the door open with his shoe, at the same time, Catarina with one final yelp, sprung away from him and ran down the hallway.

The tea kettle boiled in the kitchen below, and the women heard nothing but its whistle, not a cry of anguish, not the moan of human despair, only a dull thud, and when they heard the sound they stopped.

"What was that?" Muddy asked, wrapping a kitchen towel around the kettle's handle.

"It came from upstairs, didn't it? From Edgar's room?" Virginia asked.

"Stay here," Muddy said, and set the kettle back on the stove. She climbed the stairs quickly and when she entered the study, found her son-in-law motionless on the floor.

Above him, hung from the ceiling with garrote wire was a thin dress with a silk waist band. There was dried blood—or so it appeared—on the collar—and a note pinned there.

Muddy stared up in disbelief. She began immediately to tend to her dear Eddy, trying to rouse him, calling down to Virginia for smelling salts kept in the cupboard.

By the time she passed the vial by his nostrils a second time, the sharp ammonia brought him around and he half-sat in a state of dulled consciousness.

Virginia stood and stared at the dress. "What does this possibly mean?" she asked.

"It's an omen," Maria said. "We must arrange to have the police brought in," she added.

Virginia seemed confused. "But the police—the police were here when we were gone to the theatre. How could anyone have gotten in to hang this hideous thing?"

*   *   *

That was exactly the question Reynold asked McGurdy when he arrived with his detail.

Everyone met in the reading room, everyone but Poe. McGurdy sent one of his men up to detach the dress and it now lay on a carpet in the reading room.

"And where is the precious poet?" McGurdy asked.

"He's taken to bed, and in a deep sleep," Maria said.

"Well, wake him, and get him down here," McGurdy demanded.

"That is out of the question," Maria said.

"Why so?"

"He's been sedated. Even if aroused, he could not be expected to be coherent," she replied.

McGurdy paused a moment as if he did not quite know what to do with the information he was given. He cleared his throat. "Now you say you were out all evening?"

"Yes," Muddy said, "all of us."

"Are you sure? Maybe you had left Mr. Poe behind. Could that have happened?"

"No," she replied. "And we were seen by others at the theatre."

"I see," McGurdy said. "How was it that you visited the theatre in the first place may I ask?"

"It was a gift—from Mr. Graham, the publisher."

With that, McGurdy rose, "And where might we find this publisher?"

Soon as McGurdy's assistant jotted down Graham's address, Reynold stepped up and said, "Mr. Graham is a dear friend, and never one who would have visited this atrocity on Edgar—or his family."

"We're not sure of that," McGurdy said, then dispatched two of his officers to question Graham at his home.

Reynold bent over, close to the dress, examining it. "This gown—rumpled and unpresentable as it is—is familiar."

He looked up at McGurdy as if he might give some confirmation, and when none came, Reynold reached for the note pinned to the collar and stopped. He looked up again, "May I?" he asked McGurdy.

"Give it to me," McGurdy said, and then after reading it silently, placed it on the table for everyone to see.

> *A Third will fill this dress,*
> *And will be a sorrowful sight,*
> *With more to come,*
> *One by one, Death has no rest,*
> *Until Pride which has done them all*
> *Itself becomes undone.*

"Now Reynold," he said, "explain yourself. Whatever did you mean when you said this article of clothing had the look of familiarity?

"If I'm not mistaken, it is the same worn by the last victim. Here, you can see bits of debris still in the fibers from having it, and the body that once occupied it, drawn over difficult terrain. Surely, you must recall it when we first saw it at Fairmount Park by the skating inlet."

"If that's the case, then I think it best to pay a visit to our dear Dr. Warren," McGurdy said. "And you Reynold, since you have the clever eye, may accompany Perkins here to ascertain how it was that such a garment—in which our most recent victim was delivered to the medical examiner—came from the office of the medical examiner to the Spring Garden House."

"And your posts?" Reynold asked, "Where were they this night?"

"I spoke to each of them before I came in. They were at each door, all three, without exception."

"And none left, not for a minute, maybe to converse with another at another door leaving his entry unguarded?"

"I have their word," McGurdy said.

"Their word," Reynold repeated with sarcasm. "I wonder what their *word* is worth?"

"Whatever's on your mind, say it then," McGurdy said.

"Have your posts, all three, come to this room and remove their tunics."

"What? I'll do no such thing."

At this point, Perkins stepped over, cupped his hand and whispered in McGurdy's ear.

"That can't be. You must be mistaken," McGurdy said then stepped back.

"Then put my claim to the test," Perkins said. "That's the only way we'll know."

Faced with the possibility that McGurdy had sworn followers of Arcton's Brotherhood in his own force, among his own men, he said, "All right then. Call them in, but be quick about it," then turned to

Virginia and Maria. "Ladies, certainly you will understand if I ask you to excuse yourselves from our assembly."

With the women gone, McGurdy stood facing his three officers.

"Remove your uniforms—jackets only," he announced.

The officers turned to each other, stunned. One looked up to the ceiling; another put his hands on his hips and sighed, the third stepped forward: "Sir, may we ask the meaning of this exercise?"

"Meaning is mine to know," McGurdy said. "Your duty now is to do as you're told."

Reluctantly, each man unbuttoned his tunic, removed it, folding it over his arm.

Each wore a white undershirt, but they were not similar. Two were long-sleeved, one was not. McGurdy began by inspecting the arms of the officer who stood before him, his arms exposed. Nothing.

"Now you two," McGurdy said. "Take off your shirts."

Again, with reluctance the men did as they were instructed. One's arms were unmarked, the other's had the tattooed chain of Arcton's symbols on his bicep.

McGurdy turned to a pair of officers he had brought with him and said, "Take this man down to the ward and place him in detention for questioning."

*　　*　　*

After the room had cleared; McGurdy and Perkins had gone with the rest of the detail; Virginia and Maria were safe in their rooms upstairs where they attempted sleep, and when that was impossible, took a popular sleeping aid, a tablet of ground valerian root, poppy seed and chamomile.

Two officers remained downstairs. Their job was to protect

the property of the crime itself, which at this point was the theft and the illegal display of an item of evidence in an ongoing investigation.

They carefully folded the dress that had been the last worn by Jane Stanard, and placed it in a sealed police evidence bag to return it to the ward's vault where it should have been safely stored before the incident.

Soon as the officers left, Reynold began pacing the floor, his head bowed, hands clasped behind his back, deep in thought.

I didn't want to interrupt him, but there was something on my mind as well, something that couldn't wait.

"Look here," I blurted out, "Once my purpose here has been completed, and I can only hope it will be successful, please don't consider me as an—an—associate of some kind. You already have one of those, a most competent one I might add, in Alana."

I may have well been talking to myself at that point for he had suddenly left the room. He was down the hall when Alana approached him and they motioned me over.

Alana was beaming. "This is just what we've been hoping for," she began, then placed an outstretched hand in front of her. From her palm there issued a blue electric projection that I could only describe as photovoltaic in nature. Before us, images took form, visual emanations far beyond what I knew to be the cutting edge of modern holography. For now—and for lack of a better explanation—I could only call it paraholographic.

*   *   *

"You see before you," Alana said, "vignettes I've selected from the past several encounters between Frances Osgood and Rufus Griswold.

Each was a carefully arranged rendezvous—" here she paused, and turned my way, "we might call it a date," she said.

"In our time," I added.

"Yes," Alana replied. "But now *this*—" and her hand swept out as before to the image of Fanny and Rufus Griswold, "*is* our time, Dorn. None other."

Once Alana had made this clear, she continued, "Francis arranged to 'accidently' run into Griswold in the theatre lobby during the intermission of a recent play. She was demure as always, and managed to suggest another meeting." Alana paused, and we could hear the conversation between Fanny and Rufus among the background ruffle of skirts and long coats of other theatre goers moving about speaking in polite whispers.

"And may I be so bold to ask how you might be occupying your days now," she asked.

Rufus regarded her carefully. "Oh Fanny, you want to know about my literary projects. Maybe if I'm preparing another anthology," he said coyly.

"Why yes. Are you?"

"There's always something to steal away the public readers' attention," he smiled.

Fanny noticed the crowd begging to thin; people were returning to their seats; the intermission was almost over.

"I would very much like to discuss your new ventures at a more convenient time."

Rufus picked up on this immediately, suggesting another meeting. "I have an appointment at—" and here he mentioned the name of a famous restaurant which was considered better than Delmonico's in New York, especially for its French cuisine—Fanny loved French cuisine "—with two gentlemen agents, to discuss a reading tour for the writers they represent to promote a new literary series. However, once our conversation has ended, and I've seen my guests off, you could join me for a glass of sherry, and perhaps one of their delightful desserts," he smiled.

Fanny returned his smile, lifted the back of her hand which he took gracefully, and the couple returned to their respective seats to view the concluding act of the performance.

The images dissolved with a wave of Alana's hand. "I thought for a moment Frances may have had a chance of succeeding, but as it's turning out she may be having the tables turned on her, so to speak." With another motion of her hand, we could see the couple at the restaurant as Griswold suggested, seated together after his gentlemen guests had left.

"Among your many projects," Fanny was saying, "I've heard you are considering another attempt at *The Stylus*."

"You heard correctly," Griswold said. He paused a moment, and before Fanny could begin to plead Poe's case, he said, "In fact, there might be something you could help me with, and of course, in return, I would favor a submission from you for my forthcoming, *American Anthology of Poetry and Critical Voices*.

Fanny looked down, pretending to be taken off guard by his suggestion. "Why that would be so kind of you. I don't deserve—"

Griswold reached across the table and placed his hand over hers. "You deserve everything, and the best of it at that," he said trying to contain his enthusiasm.

"But you see, Fanny, our mutual friend, one you may know better than I, that is our dear Edgar, is dragging his feet. He's slow to agree to the generous terms set forth by our benefactors, and to that end you, having influence with him, might assure him of our good intentions and the noteworthiness of the enterprise. For this, I would happily include you in the new anthology, and with the help of those same gentlemen I met before you arrived here this evening, arrange a regional reading tour for you, and you alone, to include the city," and here, Alana explained to us standing by, "by the city, Griswold means New York."

Francis lowered her gaze. She slowly slid her hand away from under his; lifted the napkin from her lap and brought it to her lips. "Why I—I don't know what to say."

"Say nothing for now," he advised. "Give it some time. You could convince Poe to join our efforts. It would make a new man of him. It may even help the quality of Virginia's care. God knows it would help him and Muddy from becoming a public disgrace. Poverty is never romantic or lovely. It is a raw, shameful state. Convince him, Fanny. I know you could."

"If I should fail. What then? He is obstinate, as you know. He has his ideals and he abides by them. Perhaps you might revisit *his* terms, although I understand they are unacceptable to you as yours are to his."

"You won't fail," Griswold assured her. "I know you won't. There's too much at stake."

The scene faded, then went dark.

Reynold spoke up, "Ah, there, you see it? There it is, Griswold is hinting at extortion. 'There's too much at stake,' indeed. Francis Osgood herself might be *at stake*."

"This meeting didn't turn out as Francis had planned," Alana said, "but Francis did acquire the role of mediator. We can say that, can't we? Isn't that cause for hope?"

"Agreed," Reynold replied, "but mediator to what? Poe will never concede. And as for Griswold, he can't separate himself from Arcton; not from his wealth or his power, or for that matter, what he might become in the future, especially with the power of *The Stylus* behind him. Griswold's profits would be immeasurable. He would be the envy of the devil himself.

*   *   *

"Fenn," Dr. Warren called out, "Fenn Dawkins, get in here!"

The coroner was agitated. When the young intern showed up at his office door out of breath, Dr. Warren said, "These gentlemen"—he gestured to several individuals seated in his office; Chief McGurdy, Perkins, and two other officers—"are here to trace the whereabouts of the second victim's attire, that of the deceased, Jane Stanard."

Fenn seemed wary. His eyes darted from us back to Dr. Warren then to us again.

"Did you remove her clothing?" Warren asked.

"I did so, Sir, and in the manner prescribed for those in our care."

"Did you surrender her dress to the authorities?"

"Yes, I did, while they waited. There were two of them. Two officers."

"I see. And did you file the receipt as is customary."

"I did, yes."

"Retrieve it then," Dr. Warren directed.

The intern fumbled for his keys at the end of a chain in his vest pocket, then left the room and went down the hall to a file cabinet.

While he was locating Stanard's records, Dr. Warren said, "You've speculated, I suppose on just how that article of clothing found its way into Poe's study."

"We have indeed," McGurdy replied, then looked about the room indifferently.

"And that would not include this office, I trust," Dr. Warren persisted.

"That remains to be seen," McGurdy said. Then thought a moment. "Just how long has Mr. Dawkins been in your employ."

"Long enough for me to know he would be incapable of complicity in this matter," Dr. Warren said.

"You seem confident," McGurdy replied. "No reservations, then?"

"None. Ah, here we will find out," Dr. Warren said as Fenn entered the room with a file in his hand.

He went rapidly through the reports, and locating a simple form, said, "Here, here it is," and held it out to Dr. Warren.

It was snatched away by McGurdy. "I'll take that," he said. "I see your receipts are numbered. I would think you would keep a log. Do you?"

"Yes, we do as a matter of fact," Dr. Warren said.

McGurdy looked suspiciously at Fenn Dawkins. He held out the paper. "Did you make this up, boy?"

"No sir."

"You did not surrender Miss Stanard's attire to someone else, or place it elsewhere?"

"No sir. I swear."

"This document," McGurdy said, "bears the name of an officer with whom I am unfamiliar." He held out the paper to Perkins. "Know this man?"

*   *   *

Soon as he arrived at the Ward's Headquarters, McGurdy threw off his long coat over a worn leather sofa in his office and called for his desk clerk.

"Here," he said, waving the receipt, "I want you to find the man who signed this."

The officer looked down at the document. "It bears the signature of Alden Scott."

"He should be on patrol in the district south of Old Town," Perkins spoke up, then realizing he might be embarrassing McGurdy, smiled awkwardly.

"I want to see him here at once," McGurdy said.

The desk clerk went to the registration area and summoned a runner, then gave him a hastily-written note. "You are to deliver this message to Officer Alden Scott, then accompany him to the station. Is that understood?"

The boy shook his head and stood there, note in hand.

"Well, what are you waiting for?"

The boy looked up as if pleading . . .

"Oh, is it compensation then? Yes, you'll receive compensation once you've completed your task. Now off with you."

McGurdy shut his office door quietly and motioned Perkins to take a seat. McGurdy pulled up a chair close to him and looked directly into his eyes.

"Did you follow up on Mr. Graham, the friend of the Poe family who generously gifted them with theatre tickets the night the dead woman's dress was hung in that deranged poet's room?"

"I did, Sir," Perkins replied.

"And what did you learn?"

"His was a goodwill gesture, and that is all. I cannot see how he could be implicated in any of this. He has made it known he is no friend of Arcton or his clan, and cares for the principles of equal opportunity that we all value."

"I see," McGurdy said. "Has the officer that stood watch, the one we suspect of placing the garment in Poe's study, has he been interrogated?"

"He has, and unfortunately we've learned nothing. He wants representation."

"Representation?"

"Yes, such as the law allows."

"He'll have no such thing. He is a law enforcement officer and should not be associated with any act unbefitting his station. If there are criminal charges, then he will be permitted his representation, but for now, he is accountable to me," McGurdy said. "He must explain why he should not be considered suspect of unlawful entry, criminal theft, and the staging of a threatening event."

At that moment, the boy runner burst into the outer registration area with Officer Alden Scott, who was led by the registration officer to McGurdy's office.

"Mr. Scott," McGurdy began, "do you recognized this signature," he said holding out the coroner's receipt.

"Yes Sir, I do. It is my own."

"You recall having collected the evidence described in this document?" McGurdy asked.

"The garment worn by the deceased? Yes, I do."

"And where did you take this evidence?" McGurdy continued.

"Why to this station. I turned it over to the evidence clerk for proper storage. I believe I signed his ledger as well," Scott replied.

"Then how is it that this item turned up in the home of a suspect in the Jane Stanard case?"

"I was so instructed, Sir."

"You were *instructed*? By whom?"

"By my superior."

Perkins leaned over and whispered in McGurdy's ear.

"Do tell," McGurdy said in astonishment, almost to himself. He then turned to Scott.

"For the record then, your supervisor is . . ."

"Officer Harold Weatherall."

McGurdy looked at Perkins, then back at Scott. "You may expect to be reassigned, and in the meantime you are not to communicate about our discussion to anyone, especially Officer Weatherall."

McGurdy motioned to Perkins, then said to Scott, "Follow me," and walked down the hall, turned a corner and nodded to the guard who opened a heavy iron door to the holding cells.

The walked down a few steps then stopped and peered through the bars.

McGurdy pointed to the occupant. "Officer Scott, do you know this man?"

"No, Sir, not really."

"Was he the man to whom you surrendered Jane Stanard's dress, the garment she had worn during her assault and death?"

"Yes, Sir, I believe so. I gave it to him on the night I was instructed, having signed a release on Officer Weatherall's authority from our evidence clerk."

"The same man who was posting guard at the Spring Garden House?"

"Yes, Sir. He was there, as well as two others, one stationed at each door."

"You are dismissed, Mr. Scott. You may return to your duty," McGurdy said, staying behind while the young officer left the holding area.

"You," he pointed to the inmate, "are in league with Weatherall, and Weatherall is in league with Arcton. Yours is a dim future, one you might find to be a bit more favorable should you decide to give us the information we seek; what would help this ward and its fellow officers of the law. Do you understand?"

The figure in the cell faced away, staring at the wall in silence.

Before we left the station, McGurdy stopped at the registration desk, looked at Reynold and me and said, "I assigned Sgt. Tobin to his fate when I assigned Weatherall as his liaison."

"Yes, but at the time, you had no way of knowing this," Reynold said. "It was only after his meeting with Jimmy Tobin that we suspected him."

"We?" McGurdy asked.

"Dorn and I," Reynold replied.

"And you said nothing to me? Why wouldn't you have brought this to my attention?"

"I didn't think exposing Weatherall would be putting him to his best use. Tracking him; seeing where he leads us, was the better option," Reynold said.

*   *   *

When we left the station and were out on the street making our way back to the Spring Garden House, I asked Reynold, "Why did you tell McGurdy that we didn't reveal Weatherall as an operative for Arcton when we knew from the moment I saw the band of symbols tattooed on his arm when he was changing into his uniform after meeting with Sgt. Tobin?"

"Well, my tracking explanation I gave to McGurdy wasn't bad actually. There's some merit it to it, don't you think? However, exposing Weatherall early on may have encouraged McGurdy to inspect his entire force. Actually, McGurdy, after my admittedly contemptuous remark about who is infiltrating whom, would have called a general assembly there and then for the purpose of identifying those of his officers who bear the signs of Arcton's Brotherhood, but I suspected, rather strongly, that McGurdy's mind was not so keen as to pursue my observation. But there does seem to be a growing number of officers who have loyalties to Arcton and his clan. Who among us would be prepared for a wide scale exposure of Arcton's men in the precinct's ranks, especially now?

*   *   *

Reynold walked with me until we reached the Spring Garden House, then left, saying he had business in town, which was something of a relief since I hadn't been sleeping well and thought I could retire early.

I was drifting off on that crimson sofa in the reading room when I experienced a transition, that is, I was now—like Reynold—able to travel through space and time and see what other astral bodies see. It came about this way:

Drowsy, about to enter that realm of slumber, I heard a distant commotion coming from down the hall. I rose and quietly opened the door and in my stocking feet stepped quietly in the direction of the voices. The closer I came to the kitchen area, the voices rose and fell, eventually becoming more distinct.

Poe had his greatcoat on—collar flipped up like a black flare—and was about to leave for central Philadelphia to speak with an editor, and as he opened the door, saw Muddy, her chin in her palm staring into space.

Poe softly closed the door. "What is it Mother?" he asked.

"Why nothing, Eddy. Go on about your business."

"How can I, when you are so plaintive? I've seen you often like this, why so?"

"I suppose—ever since the dress incident—I've not been myself, not that I haven't struggled to be. There's sufficient trouble in our family, as you well know, without my own concerns added to those we have already, but I'm worried for our Sissy. I'm afraid for her," she stared directly at Poe.

This took his attention and he pulled back a kitchen chair, sat, removed his greatcoat and laid it over his lap. "Yes. And exactly what is your concern?" he asked.

"We should feel as though we are protected here, especially with the new police guards that posted around the house, but it is as if we are prisoners in our own home, waiting for an execution, not knowing when it will arrive." She looked down, hesitating, tapping the top of an empty sugar bowl, "the guards did not prevent one of their own from entering our home and hanging that deadly thing in our midst." She looked at Poe directly. "Could this not happen again? Could it not have been worse?"

Poe placed his hand over Muddy's which was resting on the table. "Needless worry, Mother," he said. "Soon all of this will have its end, as all things must."

Muddy tried to smile, but it was forced. "I'm thinking of our Virginia, and her welfare. We could leave—just for the time it takes for the authorities to identify those responsible for the demise of those two helpless girls—"

"Leave?" Poe asked as if something had lodged in his throat. "Why wherever would you go? What place would be dearer than your own home, the home I've provided for you and our Virginia?"

"There's . . . there's," she looked up sheepishly, "always—"

"Ah!" Poe exclaimed. "You yourself can hardly bear to bring his name to your lips! Say it then. Say it!"

"Neilson. He *is* our cousin, Eddy. And Baltimore is far from the clamor and violence we see every day on our streets here in Philadelphia. Consider it, please, for your dear wife's sake. Griswold is behind this—this—butchery and he would take my daughter— your dear Sissy from us out of his own blind malice. He knows this would not bring you to your knees, but he may reach a point when all if futile, and act out of hatred for you, you my dear Eddy."

Poe stood and pushed his chair back with such force it struck the edge of the table. "Never," he said. "I will never consider it. You will not leave me Muddy, nor take Virginia with you. Not now, not ever. And I shall never leave you. We are a family, a family that does not need another member, especially someone who simply happens to have investments that we lack for the moment. Gather your wits. All will be well. We'll see ourselves through these dark days as we have others."

He took her shoulders in his hands, bent down and kissed her forehead, then instead of leaving, he rushed upstairs, opened a desk drawer and removed a small glass ampoule, nearly black in color, brought it to his lips, sipped ever so slightly, then returned it, closing the drawer, and locking it with a key he kept in his vest.

From this point on, I saw what Poe saw, as if I too were a part of his experience, a travelling companion, invisible and unknown to him.

He steadied himself for a moment, then sat on a bench in his study. Presently, a black bird came to the window and perched on the sill. His eyes were red, and he had a piece of string in his beak and attached to it was a tiny white pouch.

Poe must have known instinctively what this meant and rushed downstairs and out the door.

The bird, still carrying the pouch flapped its wings and flew to a nearby rooftop, then as soon as Poe approached below, he flew off again, this time to a public park about a block away, resting on a wrought iron garden gate. Just as Poe came into view, he flew off once again, and set himself on top of a church steeple. And so it went. The bird flying from one place to another, waiting for Poe to arrive, then flying off again, Poe in pursuit until they were out of town and Poe followed the bird from tree to tree, and it was becoming clear from the landscape that we were heading for "The Bottoms"—we hastily traversed the thickets; came to the embankment by Gray's Ferry, then saw those hundreds of small lights, like fireflies, signaling the life-giving fires of the homeless and the unnecessary, and soon wending our way among them—the bird flitting from one ratty shelter to another—we came to Sister Sara's shanty—or what was left of it. The bird perched on a nearby rock, the string to the little pouch dangling from its beak.

The shelter had been torn apart, its sections hauled off, used elsewhere, and its inhabitants, Sister Sara and 'Frisco Red, long gone. Other than a few scraps of torn carpet and wooden slats scattered about, it was if no one had ever occupied the spot.

The raven extended its black wings and held them wide. He dropped what he'd been carrying, and skipped over the ground to what was once the floor of the couple's rickety shack. There he pecked three times, his beak piercing the ground, then looked up. We came over and stood within inches of the great bird. He glared at us with his red eyes, and when we did not respond, or move, he repeated his behavior, pecking three times on the same spot. He then stepped back and squawked shrilly as if annoyed, and hopped back to his rock and the white pouch, where he waited, observing us.

Poe scrambled for anything to remove the layers of soil. Looking about, he found a sharp-sided piece of rumpled tin someone had discarded. Wrapping his scarf around one edge, and gripping it tightly, he used the other side to cut into the dirt in the area where the bird had led him. He scraped the soil, then drove his makeshift tool like a trowel into the ground, breaking off chunks of earth, then sat back exhausted, finding nothing.

He looked back at the bird, that raven, his guide to the witch's world. The firelights flicked in the distance around him, and he was beside himself. The bird turned its head as if to question Poe, to ask why he had not discovered what it was here for him to discover.

The raven hopped over to where Poe had been digging and jumped into the pot hole and began his pecking again. He'd peck three times then looked at Poe.

Poe brushed him away with his arm, and started removing more dirt, then finally he struck something. The bird squawked.

With bits of root and debris about it, Poe slowly removed a piece of wire attached to a piece of square wood on both ends. The wire was discolored for the most part.

No one had to tell Poe that what he held in his hands was a garrote, anymore than he had to be told that what the raven had used to lure him to this spot was the packet of the same sacred powder that could cure Viriginia, as what he once held in a packet that the wanton wind had swept out of his hands.

But the great black bird, seeing this, turned his head as if to say, 'There is no such thing as what you seek. Here, look, this pouch I tempted you with, is not what you think. And if it contained what you were once promised, it would be of no greater use than dust or ash.'

"And what am I to do with this?" Poe shook the garrote in his hands. "Am I to surrender this to the authorities, claiming it took the lives of two innocents? And what would they make of that? Tell me now."

The bird shook its feathers, looked away, then said, 'Return it to its grave, and when others give witness, tell them where it may be recovered. You will know when the time is right,' and flew up, flapped its wings as it hung stationary in the air, ascended higher, circled the abandoned camp site, then squawking as if it had achieved its purpose, flew away.

Wind came up, and with it came fog and it rolled over the landscape. It was so dense, I could not see Poe any longer, and it must have taken us up as if in a draft, as the next thing I knew I was returned to Poe's study, and there he was also, slumped on that bench, his head down, and in his opened hand, was the raven's white pouch. It must have been opened by Poe before he returned to his state, for it was filled with bits of straw, a child's marble, chips of pine cone, pieces of dead leaves—worthless but for tempting Poe to The Bottoms, the abandoned abode of Sister Sara and 'Frisco Red, and the gift of a buried garrote.

*   *   *

"We have two new visitors to the holding cell," Perkins announced to McGurdy.

"And who might they be?" McGurdy asked casually turning the pages of a garment catalogue he had been perusing for an affordable suit and top hat for his mayoral ambitions which would require public speeches and he wanted to look his best.

In answer to his question, Perkins set two ivory canes on the chief's desk.

"Arcton's men?" McGurdy quickly stowed his mail order catalogue in a drawer.

"So it would appear, but not just any of Arcton's men, we have arrested the plague of this ward. Finally, we have Cobb and Dilly in custody."

"Bravo!" McGurdy exclaimed, his eyebrows up, followed by two claps of his hands.

"And the charges?"

"Aggravated assault with homicidal intent, and breaking and entering a private residence, for starters," Perkins said.

"Indeed," McGurdy replied, stroking his chin.

Perkins reported the details: It seems the pair had been observing the comings and goings of a respectable banker who lived in one of the mansions on Highport Avenue with the intention of entering the home in his absence and looting it. They noticed no other individuals visiting the property and for the lack of other human activity concluded it was unoccupied. The banker left every morning at the same time; returned at noon apparently for lunch, then departed again and was back by late afternoon. His mother was elderly, temporarily bedridden due to a fall, and he had been caring for her for the past several months, hoping her situation would improve.

Of course, this went unnoticed by the assailants. It just so happened that on the morning of their deed, the banker having been gone a quarter of an hour—long enough for Cobb and Dilly to break in a back window and begin to pillage the place—realized he had left a loan

application file on the drawing room table where he had been review-
ing it the night before—and returned to retrieve it.

Once he entered the home, he heard a scuffle coming from an
upstairs chamber; rushed up the stairs, stopped midway, turned
back and fetched a fowling piece left to him by his father, stored in a
downstairs closet.

When he entered his mother's bedroom, Cobb was straddled over
the old lady and had his cane across her throat while Dilly was busy
emptying the contents of her jewelry boxes.

The banker surprised them both; held them at bay with his shot-
gun promising mortal harm should they attempt to move; crept
slowly over to one of the larger windows, opened it and called out to
the street for help until he was heard by a passerby and that is how
the police were brought onto the scene.

At that moment, there was a soft tap on the door of the Chief's
office. Then another.

"Yes, yes," McGurdy said hurriedly with irritation, then nodded
to Perkins to allow entry. The man who stood before them was dressed
in a business suit, white suede gloves, and a top hat that McGurdy
envied immediately.

But there were more important things on the Chief's mind.
"Can't you see the Sergeant here and I are in the middle of police
business?"

"Exactly," he said tipping his hat, and placing a calling card on
McGurdy's desk, "and that is why I am here. Gentlemen, may I have
my allotted time with my clients?"

McGurdy looked at the attorney's card, then at Perkins, as if to
ask, 'Now what do we do?' then back at their new arrival.

Sgt. Perkins spoke up: "I believe attorney privileges are war-
ranted—even for these two."

"Show Mr.—Mr.—" here he squinted at the calling card.

"Swallow," the attorney said, "Charles Swallow, III," and nodded with a smile.

"And might I ask," McGurdy said, "who you represent?"

"Why those two young men in your custody, of course—wrongly accused I should add," again, with a weak smile.

"No, no, not that," McGurdy said. "You are in the employ of someone, and I wish to know who that someone might be."

"I need not disclose that fact to you—or to anyone for that matter. It will remain confidential."

"Will it now?" McGurdy replied. "It must Arcton."

"I can tell you it isn't."

"Then you may know the same individual by a different name. Say, Billy May?"

The young attorney looked uncomfortably toward the door and said, "As I've already told you, I'm under no obligation to disclose that information."

Chief McGurdy stood. "Sergeant Perkins, show Mr. Swallow here to our visitors' room. Then I want you to escort the prisoners under double guard so they may see their representative. Inform me when this man," he said pointing to the attorney, "has vacated our building."

After an hour, Perkins returned as McGurdy asked; assured him Swallow had departed, and was about to leave the office himself when McGurdy asked about the banker's elderly mother.

He removed his note pad from his tunic and riffled through some pages. "Let's see," he said following his finger down the page, "ah here it is. She was removed from her home by orderlies who arrived from the nearest infirmary to Highport, accompanied by a nurse. She is reported to be in critical condition," he said.

*   *   *

The following morning an infirmary runner burst into the ward demanding to see Chief McGurdy.

Immediately thereafter, McGurdy called Sgt. Perkins and two guards to escort Cobb and Dilly to his office.

"Gentlemen," McGurdy began. It seems the victim—that elderly, incapacitated woman you two tried to strangle to death, has not survived the night. Have you any idea what this means?" he asked.

"We don't know nuthin'" they both said at once. Then they grinned at each other confidently.

"You will be charged with a capital offense. It could mean the death penalty," McGurdy said. "And should it go to trial, I don't suspect you will find a sympathetic jury. No, on the contrary, you will find a vengeful one. How could it be otherwise?"

Dilly spoke up: "Our legal man said we don't talk to you. We only talk to him." And again each smirked to the other knowingly.

"He will be of little use to you if you are found guilty of murder as you will surely be found. However, if you are willing to disclose information that we are interested in, perhaps we can assure you of some alteration of your sentence in good faith to the court. But I can see you're not ready for this, not now. You have time to think about it. You have murdered a defenseless invalid, an old woman. No one will have anything to say in your defense. How could they?"

As they were led back to their cell in shackles, McGurdy glimpsed Mrs. O'Dell seated in the registry room.

"What's she doing here?"

"She comes every day at this hour hoping to visit with her husband."

"What's in the basket she's carrying?"

"Baked goods."

"I see. Well, five minutes then. But she can't take that in with her, and mind you, a guard must be stand between them."

Perkins went down to monitor the visit. All went well, although when Mrs. O'Dell left her husband, just as the officer was setting the chairs back that had been pushed away from the table, she quickly whispered something in Desmond's ear, then once catching this at a glance, the officer pulled them away from each other. "Be on your way now," he said, turning her over to Perkins who led her out.

After she left, Perkins set something wrapped in a cloth towel on McGurdy's desk.

"What might this be?" he asked.

"I have no idea, but Mrs. O'Dell wanted you to have it."

He gently turned back a corner of the towel, removed a crock lid, and seeing the contents, a blueberry cobbler, let the cloth wrapping fall to the floor.

"My," exclaimed McGurdy touching the side of the bowl, "and it's still warm at that. He soon frowned however, and replacing the cover said, "But this is bribery, and I'll have none of that. Dispose of it, Perkins."

"Yes, sir, if you wish, but isn't it after the fact?"

"After the fact?" McGurdy repeated. "What do you mean?"

"I mean a bribe is something promised, usually beforehand, in exchange for a privilege, or a special consideration, an understanding between two parties, and since nothing was agreed upon—no arrangement was made—I don't know how this could be considered to be a remuneration of any kind."

"You don't say? Well . . ." McCurdy stroked the side of his face, "I see your point Perkins.

Yes, yes, I see that now. Well," he lightened up, "shall we have a go at it then?"

*   *   *

It was the morning of the big day. New Year's 1844. I don't even know if Reynold slept the night because of all the last-minute preparations for the parade. His excitement alone would have kept him awake.

I was still asleep when he burst into the reading room on his way to meet his brigade.

"How do I look?" he beamed, arms outstretched like some giant bird with many-colored feathers, a gaily painted shield in one hand and a wooden spear with an arrow head in the other; a headdress that resembled a centurion's helmet with peacock feathers, an embroidered loin cloth from waist to knees, and painted shin-covers with ancient Indian symbols bound by dyed twine that was crisscrossed from ankle to knee.

"Do I not fit the part? Am I not the essence of an Aztec Fantasy Warrior?" He spun around in circles, then abruptly stopped. "Well, Dorn, tell me, do you approve?"

"Of course, but I have no idea what I'm approving of—your silly costume, the silly event, or the fact you're participating—with passion no less—in what can only be called a wasteful frivolity."

"Not to concern yourself," he said, dismissing my remarks, then gestured widely as if pulling me toward him, "come on now, we don't want to be late."

The streets were crowded with revelers out in the sharp winter air. I left Reynold to find a vantage point, and selected a corner on the parade route situated on a slope so I had an excellent view. The Mummers rolled in waves: the Firemen's Band, the String Division, The Comics, The Wenches, all brightly costumed, waving banners, flags, some on stilts, others carrying signs, or pushing their comrades in wheel barrows! What a sight! The clamor of the crowd mixed with the noise of the Mummers and their bands was deafening.

I soon spotted Reynold dancing along the edge of the crowd with his brigade, The Fancies. He was chanting, and in a half-bent position moving as if he was the fictional ancient warrior he had fantasized. And to my surprise, following not far behind was Dr. Warren costumed as a harlequin!

Everyone was laughing and yelling and talking all at once and having a good time, when I saw a figure on the other side of the street, dressed in plain clothes, break from the crowd and run over to Reynold, who ceased his revelry soon as the figure approached him, and I could see him cupping his hand and shouting something in Reynold's ear.

Reynold immediately stepped out of his ranks, removed his headdress and eye-mask and scanned the crowd. I stepped up on my toes and waved. He saw this and ran toward me, as I then rushed toward him. He pushed me onto a sidewalk and said, "There's been a breakthrough—"

"There's been a what?" I asked, the noise drowning out his words.

He took me by the crook of the arm and we hurried down a side street and turned a corner out of the melee and uproar of the throng.

"A breakthrough," he repeated. "I just learned from one of

Lippard's men—a friend of our dear Perkins—that O'Dell has information and wants to strike an agreement with McGurdy."

"We should be on our way to the ward then," I said.

"No time for that," and ushered me aside and into the doorway of an abandoned building. With a sweep of his hand there issued from his palm a blue electric projection of the kind Alana had used on other occasions, and before us images took form—there was Perkins speaking to Chief McGurdy, and McGurdy summoning two guards to escort him down the hall of the ward to where Desmond O'Dell, leader of the Citizen's Workers League was detained in isolation.

O'Dell rose and clenched the bars of his cell as the Chief approached. "I have news of the whereabouts of George Lippard," he said, "and your undercover officer, Jimmy Tobin, who apparently reported information about Arcton's doings to the wrong person."

McGurdy considered this. "How reliable is this information?" he asked.

"It bears every certainty."

"Well, out with it then."

"There must be—conditions."

"Ah yes, of course," McGurdy mused. "State them."

"When you find my information accurate, then all charges will be dropped; my men released, my freedom restored, and all restitution and damages, material and punitive, with regard to the Chestnut Street Theatre incident will be dismissed."

"A tall order," McGurdy replied. "What you have learned—whatever that may be—others must know about. How else would you have received this report? What we can hear from you we can surely hear from others."

"They will not betray me, or our league."

"We'll see about that," McGurdy said, then turned to Sgt. Perkins, "Request warrants for every member of the Citizen's Workers League."

O'Dell put his head down as if defeated.

McGurdy turned on his heel and walked down the hallway.

"Wait," O'Dell shouted. "If I am silenced; if my men are put in custody, the discovery of George Lippard and the officer you sent on a fool's mission, will be attributed to our league, and not to this ward. I will make certain of it. Every newspaper will carry the account, and it will not include you or your fellow officers."

"What then are you suggesting?" McGurdy asked.

"If you abide by my requests—to free me and my men and to drop all charges—in exchange we will remain silent, and the public will attribute the rescue of these men to you, Chief McGurdy and to your loyal officers."

McGurdy paused to think for a moment, interrupted by a prospect he could not ignore.

"Besides," O'Dell continued, "I understand the Chief District Warden would not wish to be publically embarrassed that it was not he and his officers who located Lippard and Tobin, but the Citizen's Workers League. How would that look?"

McGurdy was still musing over the implications.

"Or," O'Dell added, "You could take the credit—and consequential rewards including popularity among the general citizenry—which is no small thing for a man with mayoral ambitions."

McGurdy walked back to the cell. "Under no conditions would there be any reference whatsoever to you or your league with regard to the liberation of those kidnapped and held against their will, is that right?"

"Yes. And you have my word."

"I'll have more than your word, Desmond O'Dell, if your promises fail. Let me consider your what you've said and I'll let you know if your proposition is acceptable."

*   *   *

On his way back to his office he was met by Mr. Swallow, who tipped his hat to McGurdy, smiled tightly, and said, "I wish to speak to your prisoners."

"You mean Cobb and Dilly?" McGurdy asked.

"Precisely. They may have a statement for you."

He was shown to the holding cell and within 15 minutes asked to be removed to the little room used for interrogation, accompanied by his clients, and asked McGurdy, and the ward's notary to be present as well.

When everyone was gathered—the room was full of officers, the accused, their representative, and two attorneys from the city prosecutor's office, the ward notary who served to write depositions and official reports—it was cramped and stuffy.

"On the advice of counsel, my clients have a statement," Swallow said. "Since the victim of the assault has not survived, it is necessary to see if some arrangement can be made to mitigate any possible conviction or subsequent sentence." Here he stopped and looked at the two young men.

"Are you so agreed?" Swallow asked.

"What's that to mean?" Cobb asked, confused.

"You must disclose everything you know about your participation in the attempted theft and assault," he clarified.

"Then what?" Dilly wanted to know.

"Let me add," McGurdy said, "it is not only the homicide, you understand, the murder you two committed, but also—"

"It was Cobb," Dilly interrupted. "He was the one who wanted to put her out," and glared at his partner.

"That may be," McGurdy said, "but you are by law both held equally responsible in this heinous act. A confession is not quite sufficient. We have enough evidence for a criminal conviction of a capital offense. We require more information about your membership and activities in Arcton's Brotherhood."

Cobb looked at Dilly; Dilly at Cobb. "That would do us in, it would," they said almost simultaneously.

"Not if such information led to Arcton's conviction," McGurdy replied.

There was silence, then Swallow addressed his clients: "If Arcton and whomever else you may expect to do you harm for your testimony against them are imprisoned, as you may expect to be yourselves, albeit for different crimes, there should be no apprehension of retaliation."

"You mean they can't get to us?" Dilly asked.

"Exactly so," Swallow replied. "In addition, we will expect a death sentence to be withdrawn from the prosecution." Here he looked up to the two lawyers present from the city prosecutor's office.

The attorneys nodded in agreement.

McGurdy turned to the ward's notary. "Let the record show the representatives of the prosecutor's office have indicated their acceptance." Then he looked at the two young men seated in shackles. "Turning state's evidence beats a hanging, boys."

Swallow rose. He checked his pocket watch, then replacing it in his vest pocket looked down at his clients. "I must excuse myself as I have other business to attend across town. Whatever you are given to sign, sign and make no quibbles about it. In this carriage, we are not in the driver's seat. What you have is the best possible bargain you can expect to receive."

"We'll be telling them everthin' then?" the prisoners asked.

"Yes, everything," Swallow replied, coughed once, covering his mouth with a gloved hand and pushed his way to the door.

"You're leaving so soon?" McGurdy replied.

"Yes, there are others in need of legal representation."

"I suppose Acton's among them?" McGurdy said.

"You mean Mr. May? Why even Mr. May might need counsel," he smiled, "especially now."

*   *   *

Sgt. Perkins remained with the ward's scribe to take the deposition from the prisoners. McGurdy, having decided to take O'Dell's offer, and in a hurry to learn the whereabouts of Lippard and Jimmy Tobin from him, forced himself to stay for a few more minutes.

The prosecutors were interested in the assault of the banker's mother and her subsequent demise, but McGury intruded. "Look here, I want to know about the other victims—Ms. White and Ms. Stanard."

Cobb and Dilly regarded each other. "You tell 'em," Cobb said to Dilly.

"No, you, you tell 'em," Dilly said to Cobb.

"No quibbling. Out with it," McGurdy raised his voice.

"All right then, the Brotherhood 's a holy thing is one thing you gotta' understand. What we did, we had to do," Cobb said, "and everybody is for one and one is for all. What was done was to drive the evil out of the body of disbelievers and others who harm the Brotherhood. You won't find a man who'll who'll say different."

"Whatever do you mean?" McGurdy asked.

"They was chained to the stone downstairs of the warehouse, they was, and two columns of caners stepped up one by one and took their strikes. What was left of 'em was put out by the Whaler," Cobb volunteered, with Dilly's consent, nodding with each statement.

"The Whaler? Who in Jesus' name is the Whaler?"

"The sea man, 'Frisco Red.'"

"And he garroted them?"

"He did. And he did it there, and then they were dragged off so you'd find 'em.

"I see," McGurdy said. "And all this was done at Arcton's bidding?"

"We was commanded, we was. All of us swore obedience, a blood oath. Canna' be undone doncha' know? And it was him it was, who made up those poems we pinned to the girls."

"Yes, well, I suspected as much," McGurdy said, looking about the room.

He turned to his officers, "before these two are returned to their cell, make sure they give the name of every man who is a member of, or has ever been associated with Arcton's blasted Brotherhood, then I want you, Sgt. Perkins, to notify the Magistrate to issue warrants of arrest for each and every one of them," and left the interrogation room.

*   *   *

Late the next morning—I was still in my robe and slippers when Alana came by—I learned of Lippard's whereabouts.

I was sitting on the edge of that crimson sofa in the reading room taking notes on recent events for future reference, when Alana burst in.

"Dorn!" she exclaimed holding a copy of the newspaper. "Here it is, what everyone's been waiting for! Lippard's been found!"

"And Tobin as well?" I asked.

"Yes, and Tobin as well! It's all here," she said half out of breath with excitement, and handed me the paper.

"Where was Reynold when this happened? Did this escape his attention?"

Alana laughed, "No, not at all. He was advising McGurdy all the time," she beamed. He suggested—more like instructed—McGurdy to take O'Dell's offer and how to get the most out of those two who are down at the ward accused on theft and homicide."

"You mean Cobb and Dilly?"

"Yes, those two." So you see Reynold's been busy; right now he's at General Hospital's intake floor looking after Lippard, making sure he recovers from his ordeal. He's been confined for so long he's become weak; he's eyesight poor for lack of light where they'd been keeping him."

"When did all this occur?" I asked.

"Early this morning," Alana said, tapping the newspaper, "read about it. It's all here. I'm on my way to the hospital now to see if I can be of assistance," and she was out the door before I could suggest going with her, and so I dressed hurriedly—putting on my trousers, buttoning my shirt while I stood over the coffee table trying to read the front page . . .

Thursday, January 4, 1844
THE PHILADELPHIAN CHRONICLE & SENTINEL

IN THE WEE HOURS of the morning a raid was conducted on the cavern deep in the rock bank of the Wissahickon where it is said that holy monk Kelpius once prayed. Public watchmen and officers from three wards, a total of 55 men, under the leadership of Chief Warden McGurdy, inspired by new-found evidence, cut their way through the under-brush, surrounded the spot, and demanded the surrender of guards and other individuals who kept George Lippard and James Tobin captive since their disappearance several months ago.

Upon their release they were brought to the Fourth Street General Hospital where they are being examined and treated. The raid did not confine itself to the Wissahickon area, and resulted in the arrest of an undisclosed number of persons associated with The Brotherhood of The Perpetual Dawn, in-cludeing its founder, Mr. William May. In that number there are reported to be several political figures and public watch-men linked to the homicides of Ms. Eliza White and Jane Stanard. Chief McGurdy was unavailable for comment at this time since it is an ongoing investigation, however reports have determined an extortion plot may have be suspect in the abduction and confinement of Lippard and Tobin and the deaths of the two women.

Due to the heroic actions of Chief Warden McGurdy and his officers, our fair city may move forward to a future with far less acrimony and violence among its citizenry.

I hurriedly left the reading room eager to get to the hospital, when I heard voices coming from the kitchen. Instead of going through the reception area, the lobby, and out the front visitor's door, I moved down the hallway, then right down another to the kitchen and there saw Muddy greeting the publisher, Graham, at the other door, the one that led from the kitchen to the garden.

"Ah, Mrs. Clemm, I'm pleased I found you at home," Graham

said, tipping his hat. "I wanted to speak with Edgar as soon as possible. He must know of the release of Lippard."

"He does," Muddy replied. "And he is beyond himself with the news of his good fortune."

"Perhaps I could have a moment with him?"

"That won't be possible, Mr. Graham, you see Eddy, soon as he heard the report, left to visit his friend at the hospital."

"I see . . ." Graham said. "Well then, let me invite you personally to a grand event, a reception on the occasion of Lippard's freedom, and what will be the redivivus of *The Stylus*. At some point I will be speaking with Lippard myself regarding its appearance, and in the meantime, I would like to leave this with you," here he gave Muddy an envelope, tipped his hat once again and said, "I hope you and your family will attend."

After Graham left, Muddy opened the envelope and found three admittance passes to a gala to be held at Philadelphia's Paramount Hall in honor of Lippard, and to celebrate his release and to announce, "A Revitalizing Enterprise for Our City."

By the time I arrived at the intake floor of the hospital it was congested with reporters, police watchmen, council members, those involved in the rescue and roughed up in the fray; nurses and physicians scurrying about trying to treat everyone at the same time. The administration had posted orderlies at the entrances to prevent more intruders. Apparently I was considered as such, and I had to stand on my toes and shout out to Reynold who was out of sight, but I imagined at Lippard's bedside. I shouted again for Graham, but one of the orderlies approached and warned me, "to quiet down, there're sick people here trying to get well and they don't need to be disturbed."

I resigned myself to turning away from the scene and going

outside. I took a seat on a marble bench in a garden area used for reflection and meditation.

Alana appeared.

"I called out for Reynold," I said. "And then I imagined myself moving through the crowd, but it didn't work."

"Yes, I know. And here I am instead. I'll have to do," she smiled. "Had you come with me I'd have gotten you through, you know. Your ability to transport your own eidolon is not always spontaneous. It takes time. You'll master it eventually."

"How is Lippard?" I asked.

"Not well, I'm afraid. His confinement has taken a toll. He looks emaciated as one might expect, but the physicians are cautiously optimistic that he will improve over the next day or two, and Reynold is there at his side."

"Tobin?" I asked.

"About the same, maybe a bit better; he's sitting up at the moment, anyway. We're all pulling for them, and I think they know this, and it may help their recovery. Is there anything else?"

"No, not really, but thanks for asking," and when I looked up, she had vanished.

I remained there long enough to see Lippard's family ushered in by some orderlies and one of McGurdy's guards.

*   *   *

I took my time getting back to the Spring Garden House; stopped to look over the wares of street vendors, paused by a fountain in which children were playing in a local park, and they scattered with their mothers and nannies when a group of thugs came through shouting obscenities—it was clear they were looking for something, or some-one to challenge.

Eventually I returned to the reading room, and to my surprise soon as I unlocked the door found Reynold seated in an overstuffed chair near an Argon lamp reading from one of Poe's collections.

"Ah, Dorn," he said when I entered. "Sorry I couldn't see you at the hospital. It was so crowded, only the families were allowed to stay any length of time. When Lippard did speak it was with great effort and only then in not much more than a whisper. When he spoke, his first words expressed concern for Poe, and when that happened, Poe stepped forth from the gathering, came to his bed-side, and embraced him as he would a long lost brother.

Of course, McGurdy and his detail were present, and he kept pestering Tobin and Lippard, wanting to know the specifics of their capture and confinement, but he became such a nuisance that the physicians wouldn't have it and demanded he leave, and return at a more favorable time when the men were in better condition."

Reynold placed the book back on the shelf and turned to me: "Let's plan on attending Graham's *soiree*, shall we? It's certain to be the event of the New Year!

*   *   *

Several weeks later—it was not yet the end of January—we set off for Paramount Hall and it famed Greek Ballroom which had been gaily decorated for the occasion.

Reynold and I waited in the lobby for Alana who accompanied Maria and Virginia, and then made sure they were seated in the front row before the dais which had a semi-circle of chairs for dignitaries and supported an elaborate lectern with Corinthian columns on either side.

Poe's women, led by Mrs. Whitman had been gathered in the back of the room, and entered in a single line to take their seats in the first row with Poe's wife and Maria.

McGurdy and Perkins occupied chairs behind the lectern, along with Desmond O'Dell, George Lippard, James Tobin, Graham, and other former investors of *The Stylus*, a few city council members, an official from the Greater Philadelphia Chamber of Commerce, and the publisher-owner of the *Chronicle & Sentinel*.

The introductions had gone to the Mayor, who was ailing, and required assistance to move from his chair on the platform to the lectern.

The audience was in continual conversation, busy with the concerns of the day; business leaders discussing prospects, animated bankers and attorneys exchanging comments, notable personages from every sector of the city.

The Mayor stood in full view, his hand clutching the edge of the rostrum to steady himself. Once everyone saw him waiting, they began to quiet down. When there was silence, he began:

"This evening it is my distinct honor to address this august congregation, and to introduce our plenary speaker, a noble Philadelphian, philanthropist, civic leader, and renowned publisher who has, at every turn, bettered our community beyond visible measure. Will you join with me in welcoming Mr. George Rex Graham . . ." and stood aside, clapping along with the entire assembly.

"Thank you, Mr. Mayor," Graham began, "Tonight we honor those who have devoted themselves to the undoing of a formidable body of citizens who were determined to undermine the welfare, and the very foundations, of our way of life. Their mission was to create rancor, discord, and wrath among the members of our city; to pit us against one another to promote an agenda of fear, and hatred, and nativism. I take no little pride in saying they are no longer able to pursue their destructive agenda, and our city has been lifted high as a result."

There were nods of agreement from the audience, and hearty shouts of "Hear, Hear!" echoed throughout the ballroom.

When the shouting died down, he began again: "Those who sought to incite violence and have taken the lives of two of our members are now—and shall forever remain—incarcerated for their crimes."

Graham removed a folded sheet from the vest pocket of his suit. "Let me now turn to a related subject, if I may. As many of you know, since my retirement I have been somewhat uneasy; admittedly I did not want the responsibilities and burdens associated with an enterprise with a circulation as large as my magazine, and yet, I did not want to leave it altogether, either. So to strike a middle ground, I transferred my interests in the periodical, and its editorship was assumed by another individual, Rufus Griswold, who led me to invest in an completely new literary endeavor, *The Stylus*, conceived by Mr. Poe," he paused, looked over his glasses, nodded in acknowledgment to Poe who stood far back in a corner of the great hall, his arms crossed, quietly observing the occasion. "However, I did not know the price that venture would extract—creating divisions in our community with hate mongering and vitriol.

Since Mr. Lippard has returned to us, I have spoken with him at length—and with Mr. Poe as well—and we are agreed that my capital will be redirected; joined with that of our dear brother, George Lippard, and that will truly secure the success of *The Stylus* under its new publisher and chief editor," he opened his palm, extended his arm, "Mr. Edgar Allan Poe. It is certain to be the most culturally refined, and richest literary publication in America!"

The audience burst into sustained applause.

Eventually, Graham had to hold up his hands in an effort to calm the uproar so that he could continue: "Moreover, the monthly column that Arcton would have used to propagandize his unholy brotherhood and incite our city, will now feature the work of Mr. George Lippard; a series that will capture the attention of all, and improve the cultural life in every household, and every citizen, to be called 'The Philadelphian Worker'".

Here, everyone seated on the dais behind him, led by Desmond O'Dell, rose and cheered in approval.

Once this died down, Graham returned his sheet of notes to his coat pocket, and said, "Please let me allow you to return to your evening, and to thank you again for your gracious presence in this great hall. I hope this will remain a night that we will all remember fondly, and with great hope: truly a return to mutual respect and affection in our city of brotherly love once more.

The orchestra has offered to entertain requests; please avail yourselves of the libations and *hors d'oeuvres* prepared especially for this occasion, available in the adjacent rooms."

The crowd, discussing the event and its implications, broke off in groups headed toward the various tables that were set out, while Reynold, Alana and I went off to the lobby.

McGurdy approached Reynold, "It's seems all tidy, doesn't it?" he asked. "But while we've established motive and have the criminals in hand, we do not have the man Cobb and Dilly saw deliver the *coup de grace*, the Whaler man."

"He probably put out to sea," Reynold said, "soon as he received word that his Cobb and Dilly were apprehended and turned state's evidence."

"Yes, and we don't have the murder weapon, either," McGurdy added.

"The garrote?" I asked. "It's location might give credence to his guilt . . ."

At this moment, Poe, as he was leaving, paused and looked in our direction. When he caught McGurdy's attention, he pointed out the window of the lobby door, and there perched on a the black branch of a winter tree, was the raven.

"Now what does *that* mean?" McGurdy asked with irritation, as Poe disappeared through the door with his family, and out into the night.

"It means you should follow the bird," I said.

"Nonsense," McGurdy replied.

"Take a detail and follow him and you will have your murder weapon," I said.

"Do it," Reynold concurred, "and do it now."

When McGurdy summoned two officers and left the lobby, Alana spoke up: "Poe has now achieved the success—and the societal acceptance, even acclaim—that he had always yearned for," she said, "and moving forward, Virginia and Muddy will be able live in the best of circumstances with every possible comfort. Surely, they deserve that much."

"Agreed," Reynold said, "and if Poe's old rival, Griswold, should ever find his way out of prison for extortion and complicity in a capital offense, he will not be accepted anywhere, or by anyone. His life will be one of shame and public humiliation."

Then he turned to me. He placed a hand on my shoulder. "Well, Dorn, are you ready for your return to your own time? Are you prepared to recast Poe's image, and reveal your own experiences in this dimension? In short, are you ready to rewrite history, and contribute to a new understanding of our purpose in a parallel reality—the one in which you've played such a vital part?"

I had with me the essay Poe had penned, the artifact that would be the evidence for my narrative. Holding it firmly in my hand, I said, "I believe so. But I would like to know, should the occasion arise, if I may call out to you."

Reynold looked at me, then at Alana, who spoke for him: "You may call out to Reynold only in dire emergency, in a life-threatening situation, otherwise, you'll have to deal with me," she smiled.

"And that begins now," Reynold said. "Alana, would you please be so kind as to take Dr. Dorn and show him back to the place from which he came to us? I'm sure there are many who have missed him dearly and will celebrate his return and his revolutionary message."

BORNEM, A MYTHIC PROPHECY

So much had the storm gathered in strength and force through the evening that by early night, I hesitated to keep my promise, choosing—what choice I had—to remain within the warm confines of my home and hearth, rather than venture out into the rain and wind to meet the one person in the world who could save me from the horrors that had been predicted to befall me.

As I had financial commitments in town earlier that week and went by foot to resolve them with a local creditor, the stranger stepped out from between two buildings and stood directly in my path. He—I say he—but cloaked in dark dress, the features of the face all but obscured—could have been anyone, or *anything*—spoke with a voice unlike ever I had heard warning me of disaster. He could not protect me, only assure me that what he predicted would pass surely as what he had foretold others.

I suspected this dark image, speaking darker still, might be a specter of yet some other thing, and that his sole purpose was to inform mortals of their destiny.

While he spoke, I could not move, or dared not. It was though I was fixed by his presence, unable to stir, or speak myself. There was no question of his sincerity, or his power. Many questions were on my lips, and went unheard, vanished with this dim image. What was I left with? A set of directions; I was to go to an appointed place at an appointed day, and meet with someone who could act as my second; assist me in avoiding certain disaster.

That was my business the night I fought the wind and rain to find the prefixed place where I could change my fate. If I did not appear, ineffable horrors would befall me.

The place was an old inn in the west district of the city, frequented by a few employees of a counting house, typesetters and proofers from the newspaper, and the remainder of the patrons were of the working class; diggers and railway loaders. I went immediately to the proprietor asking for the name given me by the specter. He summoned me to the back of the establishment, opening the lock of a door leading to an empty room. It was a place for storage, or so it seemed with iron rings along the walls to open closets that contained what? Would I ever know, fearing what I would find, I did not dare go near.

'There,' he told me, 'you may wait until Bornem comes.'

He lit the oil lamp on the table, and when he left, I could hear the key turn in the lock. I was secured for my guest, and began to measure the time of light left by the oil in the lamp. Surely the owner would return. He knew why I was here. Had he not done this before for others? A servant of fate?

I was there for how long I knew not. The light was beginning to dim, the room grew cold, and where was this person who would explain how I could avoid the certain despair that the Future surely held for me? The wick began to flicker casting odd shadows on the walls—and a thin dark thing slipped as if from the edge of one of the closet doors, and became a figure not unlike the one I saw standing before me, obscuring my path.

"Are you Bornem?" I asked.

The figure remained silent, and what followed instead was a tremor, a shudder of the body, then as if from this form, wave after wave issued forth; I could feel it wash over me, a speechless communication in which I understood everything clearly, everything I was supposed to understand—no—obligated—to understand.

The prophecy was so much the sum of a wordless series of emanations, and such clarity as I had never known: to spare myself and my family of untold suffering, it was necessary to walk the same path at the same time day after day, every day for the remainder of my life, and to greet the specter there between the buildings as he would appear at that moment of my approach, and I would acknowledge his presence. *Acknowledge his presence*! I was the chosen one for this task, greater than any other, so this poor creature—half-life tho' it was—could be brought into greater commerce with the world, otherwise he would remain only a hollow phantom having no larger self. I agreed—how could I not? This stranger would become a thing unto himself, a form, a life! For he had no hope of any other but through the assurance of his truth from mortals.

Once the prophecy was delivered, I heard the proprietor turn the key in the door, and at the same time, Bornem retracted first into shadow, then to nothing at all, and I was released.